HANS ANDERSEN
His Classic Fairy Tales

Hans Christian Andersen

Hans Christian Andersen was born in Odense, Denmark in 1805, the son of a poor shoemaker. At the age of fourteen, without a penny to his name, he set off to make his fortune in Copenhagen. There he found patrons in theatres and in the salons of the rich, including the king, and it was his new guardians who helped him acquire the schooling he had missed. He chose to live by his pen and wrote poems, plays and libretti for adults, but it was not until he was in his thirties, with his reputation secure, that he embarked on the form of writing that was to bring him enduring fame: the fairy tale. Andersen wrote more than 150 of these stories and many of them, such as *The Ugly Duckling*, *The Little Mermaid* and *The Emperor's New Clothes* have become part of the fabric of childhood. They were, Andersen said, "My gift to the world." He died in 1875.

Michael Foreman

Michael Foreman is one of the most highly acclaimed illustrators in Britain today. He has twice won both the Kate Greenaway Medal for outstanding children's book illustration and the Francis Williams Memorial Prize (awarded by the Victoria & Albert Museum). Recently he was the winner of the Smarties Book Prize and he has also won the Kurt Maschler "Emil" Award, the Federation of Children's Book Groups' Children's Book Award, and the Bologna Book Fair Graphic Prize for Youth. He has illustrated several other Gollancz Children's Classics, including *A Christmas Carol*, *Shakespeare Stories*, volumes I and II, and *The Arabian Nights*. He lives in London and Cornwall.

Erik Christian Haugaard

Erik Haugaard, a distinguished children's author in his own right, was born in Copenhagen in 1923. He h ʾ   ᵈ ᵒⁿ the subject of Hans Christian Andersen on both sides of the

HANS ANDERSEN

His Classic Fairy Tales

From the translation by
ERIK HAUGAARD

Illustrated by
MICHAEL FOREMAN

GOLLANCZ CHILDREN'S PAPERBACKS

LONDON

First published in Great Britain 1976
by Victor Gollancz Ltd
First published in Gollancz Children's Paperbacks 1985

This new edition 1995 by Victor Gollancz
An imprint of the Cassell Group
Wellington House, 125 Strand, London WC2R 0BB

Translation copyright © Erik Christian Haugaard 1974
Illustrations copyright © Michael Foreman 1976

A catalogue record for this book is
available from the British Library

ISBN 0 575 06210 X

Printed in Spain by Bookprint SL

Contents

	Page
The Tinderbox	11
The Nightingale	19
The Princess and the Pea	29
The Swineherd	32
The Ugly Duckling	38
The Dung Beetle	48
The Snowman	57
The Snow Queen	63
The Darning Needle	94
The Steadfast Tin Soldier	98
The Little Match Girl	103
Little Claus and Big Claus	107
The Emperor's New Clothes	119
The Wild Swans	125
The Old House	140
The Little Mermaid	149
The Red Shoes	171
Inchelina	178

List of Illustrations

	Page
There sat the dog with eyes as big as millstones	13
Even the fisherman would stop to rest when he heard the nightingale	21
Only a real princess could be so sensitive!	30
"I have never heard a more exquisite composition"	35
Towards evening he came upon a poor little hut	43
"Golden shoes!" repeated the dung beetle crossly	51
All day long the snowman gazed through the window	61
By now they were flying high up in the clouds	69
They heard the wolves howl and the ravens cry	85
He sat arranging pieces of ice into patterns	89
"Give me your passport!"	101
She lifted the little girl in her arms	105
"I'll give your horse gee up!" screamed Big Claus	109
"But he doesn't have anything on!"	123
They flew one after the other	131
"I can't stand it here," wailed the tin soldier	143
He would have drowned, had the little mermaid not saved him	155
Every minute, the witch put something different into the cauldron	163
Dance she did, out through the city gates and into the dark forest	175
Now the leaf raced down the stream	183
The swallow flew high up into the air	187

HANS ANDERSEN

His Classic Fairy Tales

The Tinderbox

A soldier came marching down the road: Left . . . right! Left . . . right! He had a pack on his back and a sword at his side. He had been in the war and he was on his way home. Along the road he met a witch. She was a disgusting sight, with a lower lip that hung all the way down to her chest.

"Good evening, young soldier," she said. "What a handsome sword you have and what a big knapsack. I can see that you are a real soldier! I shall give you all the money that you want."

"Thank you, old witch," he said.

"Do you see that big tree?" asked the witch, and pointed to the one they were standing next to. "The trunk is hollow. You climb up to the top of the tree, crawl into the hole, and slide deep down inside it. I'll tie a rope around your waist, so I can pull you up again when you call me."

"What am I supposed to do down in the tree?" asked the soldier.

"Get money!" answered the witch and laughed. "Now listen to me. When you get down to the very bottom, you'll be in a great passageway where you'll be able to see because there are over a hundred lamps burning. You'll find three doors; and you can open them all because the keys are in the locks. Go into the first one; and there on a chest, in the middle of the room, you'll see a dog with eyes as big as teacups. Don't let that worry you. You will have my blue checked apron; just spread it out on the floor, put the dog down on top of it, and it won't do you any harm.

11

Open the chest and take as many coins as you wish, they are all copper. If it's silver you're after, then go into the next room. There you'll find a dog with eyes as big as millstones; but don't let that worry you, put him on the apron and take the money. If you'd rather have gold, you can have that too; it's in the third room. Wait till you see that dog, he's got eyes as big as the Round Tower in Copenhagen; but don't let that worry you. Put him down on my apron and he won't hurt you; then you can take as much gold as you wish."

"That doesn't sound bad!" said the soldier. "But what am I to do for you, old witch? I can't help thinking that you must want something too."

"No," replied the witch. "I don't want one single coin. Just bring me the old tinderbox that my grandmother forgot the last time she was down there."

"I'm ready, tie the rope around my waist!" ordered the soldier.

"There you are, and here is my blue checked apron," said the witch.

The soldier climbed the tree, let himself fall into the hole, and found that he was in the passageway, where more than a hundred lights burned.

He opened the first door. Oh! There sat the dog with eyes as big as teacups glaring at him.

"You are a handsome fellow!" he exclaimed as he put the dog down on the witch's apron. He filled his pockets with copper coins, closed the chest, and put the dog back on top of it.

He went into the second room. Aha! There sat the dog with eyes as big as millstones. "Don't keep looking at me like that," said the soldier good-naturedly. "It isn't polite and you'll spoil your eyes." He put the dog down on the witch's apron and opened the chest. When he saw all the silver coins, he emptied the copper out of his pockets and filled both them and his knapsack with silver.

Now he entered the third room. That dog was big enough to frighten anyone, even a soldier. His eyes were as large as the Round Tower in Copenhagen and they turned around like wheels.

"Good evening," said the soldier politely and saluted, for such a dog he had never seen before. For a while he just stood looking at it; but finally he said to himself, "Enough of this!" Then he put the dog down on the witch's apron and opened up the chest.

"God preserve me!" he cried. There was so much gold that there was enough to buy the whole city of Copenhagen; and all the gingerbread men, rocking horses, riding whips, and tin soldiers in the whole world.

Quickly the soldier threw away all the silver coins that he had in his pockets and knapsack and put gold in them instead. He also filled his cap, and he stuffed so many coins in his boots he could hardly walk. Then he put the dog back on the chest, and slammed the door behind him.

"Pull me up, you old witch!" he shouted up through the hollow tree.

"Have you got the tinderbox?" she called back.

"Right you are, I have forgotten it," he replied honestly, and went back to get it. The witch hoisted him up and again he stood on the road; but now his pockets, knapsack, cap, and boots were filled with gold and he felt quite differently.

"Why do you want the tinderbox?" he asked.

"Mind your own business," answered the witch crossly. "You have got your money, just give me the tinderbox."

"Rubbish!" said the soldier. "Tell me what you are going to use it for, right now; or I'll draw my sword and cut off your head."

"No!" replied the witch firmly; so he chopped her head off. And when she lay there dead, he put all his gold in her apron, which he tied into a bundle, and threw over his shoulder. The tinderbox he dropped into his pocket; and off to town he went.

The town was nice, and the soldier went to the nicest inn, where he asked to be put up in the finest room and ordered all the things he liked to eat best for his supper, because now he had so much money that he was rich.

The servant who polished his boots thought it was very odd that a man so wealthy should have such worn-out boots. But the soldier hadn't had time to buy anything yet; the next day he bought boots and clothes that fitted his purse. And the soldier became a refined gentleman. People were eager to tell him all about their town and their king, and what a lovely princess his daughter was.

"I would like to see her," said the soldier.

"But no one sees her," explained the townfolk. "She lives in a copper castle, surrounded by walls, and towers, and a moat. The king doesn't dare allow anyone to visit her because it has been foretold that she will marry a common soldier, and the king doesn't want that to happen."

"If only I could see her," thought the soldier, though it was unthinkable.

The soldier lived merrily, went to the theatre, kept a carriage so he could drive in the king's park, and gave lots of money to the poor. He remembered well what it felt like not to have a penny in his purse.

He was rich and well dressed. He had many friends; and they all said that he was kind and a real cavalier; and such things he liked to hear. But since he used money every day and never received any, he soon had only two copper coins left.

He had to move out of the beautiful room downstairs, up to a tiny one in the garret, where he not only polished his boots himself but also mended them with a large needle. None of his friends came to see him, for they said there were too many stairs to climb.

It was a very dark evening and he could not even buy a candle. Suddenly he remembered that he had seen the stub of a candle in the tinderbox that he had brought up from the bottom of the hollow tree. He found the tinderbox and took out the candle. He struck the flint. There was a spark, and in through the door came the dog with eyes as big as teacups.

"What does my master command?" asked the dog.

"What's this all about?" exclaimed the soldier. "That certainly was an interesting tinderbox. Can I have whatever I want? Bring me some money," he ordered. In less time than it takes to say thank you, the dog was gone and back with a big sack of copper coins in his mouth.

Now the soldier understood why the witch had thought the tinderbox so valuable. If he struck it once, the dog appeared who sat on the chest full of copper coins; if he struck it twice, then the dog came who guarded the silver money; and if he struck it three times, then came the one who had the gold.

The soldier moved downstairs again, wore fine clothes again, and had fine friends, for now they all remembered him and cared for him as they had before.

One night, when he was sitting alone after his friends had gone, he thought, "It is a pity that no one can see that beautiful princess. What is the good of her beauty if she must always remain behind the high walls and towers of a copper castle? Will I never see her? . . . Where is my tinderbox?"

He made the sparks fly and the dog with eyes as big as teacups came. "I know it's very late at night," he said, "but I would so like to see the beautiful princess, if only for a minute."

Away went the dog; and faster than thought he returned with the sleeping princess on his back. She was so lovely that anyone would have known that she was a real princess. The soldier could not help kissing her, for he was a true soldier.

The dog brought the princess back to her copper castle; but in the morning while she was having tea with her father and mother, the king and queen, she told them that she had had a very strange dream that night. A large dog had come and carried her away to a soldier who kissed her.

"That's a nice story," said the queen, but she didn't mean it.

The next night one of the older ladies in waiting was sent to watch over the princess while she slept, to find out whether it had only been a dream, and not something worse.

The soldier longed to see the princess so much that he couldn't bear it, so at night he sent the dog to fetch her. The dog ran as fast as he could, but the lady in waiting had her boots on and she kept up with him all the way. When she saw which house he had entered, she took out a piece of chalk and made a big white cross on the door.

"Now we'll be able to find it in the morning," she thought, and went home to get some sleep.

When the dog returned the princess to the castle, he noticed the cross on the door of the house where his master lived; so he took a piece of white chalk and put crosses on all the doors of all the houses in the whole town. It was a very clever thing to do, for now the lady in waiting would never know which was the right door.

The next morning the king and queen, the old lady in waiting, and all the royal officers went out into town to find the house where the princess had been.

"Here it is!" exclaimed the king, when he saw the first door with a cross on it.

"No, my sweet husband, it is here," said his wife, who had seen the second door with a cross on it.

"Here's one!"

"There's one!"

Everyone shouted at once, for it didn't matter where anyone looked: there he would find a door with a cross on it; and so they all gave up.

Now the queen was so clever, she could do more than ride in a golden carriage. She took out her golden scissors and cut out a large piece of silk and sewed it into a pretty little bag. This she filled with the fine grain of buckwheat, and tied the bag around the princess' waist. When this was done, she cut a little hole in the bag just big enough for the little grains of buckwheat to fall out, one at a time, and show the way to the house where the princess was taken by the dog.

During the night the dog came to fetch the princess and carry her on his back to the soldier, who loved her so much that now he had only one desire, and that was to be a prince so that he could marry her.

The dog neither saw nor felt the grains of buckwheat that made a little trail all the way from the copper castle to the soldier's room at the inn. In the morning the king and queen had no difficulty in finding where the princess had been, and the soldier was thrown into jail.

There he sat in the dark with nothing to do; and what made matters worse was that everyone said, "Tomorrow you are going to be hanged!"

That was not amusing to hear. If only he had had his tinderbox, but he had forgotten it in his room. When the sun rose, he watched the people, through the bars of his window, as they hurried toward the gates of the city, for the hanging was to take place outside the walls. He heard the drums and the royal soldiers marching. Everyone was running. He saw a shoemaker's apprentice, who had not bothered to take off his leather apron and was wearing slippers. The boy lifted his legs so high, it looked as though he were galloping. One of his slippers flew off and landed near the window of the soldier's cell.

"Hey!" shouted the soldier. "Listen, shoemaker, wait a minute, nothing much will happen before I get there. But if you will run to the inn and get the tinderbox I left in my room, you can earn four copper coins. But you'd better use your legs or it will be too late."

The shoemaker's apprentice, who didn't have one copper coin, was eager to earn four; and he ran to get the tinderbox as fast as he could; and gave it to the soldier.

And now you shall hear what happened after that!

Outside the gates of the town, a gallows had been built; around it stood the royal soldiers and many hundreds of thousands of people. The king and the queen sat on their lovely throne, and opposite them sat the judge and the royal council.

The soldier was standing on the platform, but as the noose was put around his neck, he declared that it was an ancient custom to grant a condemned man his last innocent wish. The only thing he wanted was to be allowed to smoke a pipe of tobacco.

The king couldn't refuse; and the soldier took out his tinderbox and struck it: once, twice, three times! Instantly, the three dogs were before him: the one with eyes as big as teacups, the one with eyes as big as millstones, and the one with eyes as big as the Round Tower in Copenhagen.

"Help me! I don't want to be hanged!" cried the soldier.

The dogs ran toward the judge and the royal council. They took one man by the leg and another by the nose, and threw them up in the air, so high that when they hit the earth again they broke into little pieces.

"Not me!" screamed the king; but the biggest dog took both the king and the queen and sent them flying up as high as all the others had been.

The royal guards got frightened; and the people began to shout: "Little soldier, you shall be our king and marry the princess!"

The soldier rode in the king's golden carriage; and the three dogs danced in front of it and barked: "Hurrah!"

The little boys whistled and the royal guards presented arms. The princess came out of her copper castle and became queen, which she liked very much. The wedding feast lasted a week; and the three dogs sat at the table and made eyes at everyone.

The Nightingale

In China, as you know, the emperor is Chinese, and so are his court and all his people. This story happened a long, long time ago; and that is just the reason why you should hear it now, before it is forgotten. The emperor's palace was the most beautiful in the whole world. It was made of porcelain and had been most costly to build. It was so fragile that you had to be careful not to touch anything and that can be difficult. The gardens were filled with the loveliest flowers; the most beautiful of them had little silver bells that tinkled so you wouldn't pass by without noticing them.

Everything in the emperor's garden was most cunningly arranged. The gardens were so large that even the head gardener did not know exactly how big they were. If you kept walking you finally came to the most beautiful forest, with tall trees that mirrored themselves in deep lakes. The forest stretched all the way to the sea, which was blue and so deep that even large boats could sail so close to the shore that they were shaded by the trees. Here lived a nightingale who sang so sweetly that even the fisherman, who came every night to set his nets, would stop to rest when he heard it, and say: "Blessed God, how beautifully it sings!" But he couldn't listen too long, for he had work to do, and soon he would forget the bird. Yet the next night when he heard it again, he would repeat what he had said the night before: "Blessed God, how beautifully it sings!"

From all over the world travellers came to the emperor's city to admire his palace and gardens; but when they heard the nightingale sing, they all declared that it was the loveliest of all. When they returned to their own countries, they would write long and learned books about the city, the palace, and the garden; but they didn't forget the nightingale. No, that was always mentioned in the very first chapter. Those who could write poetry wrote long odes about the nightingale who lived in the forest, on the shores of the deep blue sea.

These books were read the whole world over; and finally one was also sent to the emperor. He sat down in his golden chair and started to read it. Every once in a while he would nod his head because it pleased him to read how his own city and his own palace and gardens were praised; but then he came to the sentence: "But the song of the nightingale is the loveliest of all."

"What!" said the emperor. "The nightingale? I don't know it, I have never heard of it; and yet it lives not only in my empire but in my very garden. That is the sort of thing one can only find out by reading books."

He called his chief courtier, who was so very noble that if anyone of a rank lower than his own, either talked to him, or dared ask him a question, he only answered, "P". And that didn't mean anything at all.

"There is a strange and famous bird called the nightingale," began the emperor. "It is thought to be the most marvellous thing in my empire. Why have I never heard of it?"

"I have never heard of it," answered the courtier. "It has never been presented at court."

"I want it to come this evening and sing for me," demanded the emperor. "The whole world knows of it but I do not."

"I have never heard it mentioned before," said the courtier, and bowed. "But I shall search for it and find it."

But that was more easily said than done. The courtier ran all through the palace, up the stairs and down the stairs, and through the long corridors, but none of the people whom he asked had ever heard of the nightingale. He returned to the emperor and declared that the whole story was nothing but a fable, invented by those people who had written the books. "Your Imperial Majesty should not believe everything that is written. A discovery is one thing and artistic imagination something quite different; it is fiction."

"The book I have just read," replied the emperor, "was sent to me by the great Emperor of Japan; and therefore, every word in it must be the

truth. I want to hear the nightingale! And that tonight! If it does not come, then the whole court shall have their stomachs thumped, and that right after they have eaten."

"*Tsing-pe!*" said the courtier. He ran again up and down the stairs and through the corridors; and half the court ran with him, because they didn't want their stomachs thumped! Everywhere they asked about the nightingale that the whole world knew about, and yet no one at court had heard of.

At last they came to the kitchen, where a poor little girl worked, scrubbing the pots and pans. "Oh, I know the nightingale," she said, "I know it well, it sings so beautifully. Every evening I am allowed to bring some leftovers to my poor sick mother who lives down by the sea. Now it is far away, and as I return I often rest in the forest and listen to the nightingale. I get tears in my eyes from it, as though my mother were kissing me."

"Little kitchenmaid," said the courtier, "I will arrange for a permanent position in the kitchen for you, and permission to see the emperor eat, if you will take us to the nightingale; it is summoned to court tonight."

Half the court went to the forest to find the nightingale. As they were walking along a cow began to bellow.

"Oh!" shouted all the courtiers. "There it is. What a marvellously powerful voice the little animal has; we have heard it before."

"That is only a cow," said the little kitchmaid. "We are still far from where the nightingale lives."

They passed a little pond; the frogs were croaking.

"Lovely," sighed the Chinese imperial dean. "I can hear her, she sounds like little church bells ringing."

"No, that is only the frogs," said the little kitchenmaid, "but any time now we may hear it."

Just then the nightingale began singing.

"There it is!" said the little girl. "Listen. Listen. It is up there on that branch." And she pointed to a little grey bird sitting amid the greenery.

"Is that possible?" exclaimed the chief courtier. "I had not imagined it would look like that. It looks so common! I think it has lost its colour from shyness and out of embarrassment at seeing so many noble people at one time."

"Little nightingale," called the kitchenmaid, "our emperor wants you to sing for him."

"With pleasure," replied the nightingale, and sang as beautifully as he could.

"It sounds like little glass bells," sighed the chief courtier. "Look at its little throat, how it throbs. It is strange that we have never heard of it before; it will be a great success at court."

"Shall I sing another song for the emperor?" asked the nightingale, who thought that the emperor was there.

"Most excellent little nightingale," began the chief courtier, "I have the pleasure to invite you to attend the court tonight, where His Imperial Majesty, the Emperor of China, wishes you to enchant him with your most charming art."

"It sounds best in the green woods," said the nightingale; but when he heard that the emperor insisted, he followed them readily back to the palace.

There every room had been polished and thousands of little golden lamps reflected themselves in the shiny porcelain walls and floors. In the corridors stood all the most beautiful flowers, the ones with silver bells on them; and there was such a draught from all the servants running in and out, and opening and closing doors, that all the bells were tinkling and you couldn't hear what anyone said.

In the grand banquet hall, where the emperor's throne stood, a little golden perch had been hung for the nightingale to sit on. The whole court was there and the little kitchenmaid, who now had the title of Imperial Kitchenmaid, was allowed to stand behind one of the doors and listen. Everyone was dressed in their finest clothes and they all were looking at the little grey bird, towards which the emperor nodded very kindly.

The nightingale's song was so sweet that tears came into the emperor's eyes; and when they ran down his cheeks, the little nightingale sang even more beautifully than it had before. His song spoke to one's heart, and the emperor was so pleased that he ordered his golden slipper to be hung around the little bird's neck. There was no higher honour. But the nightingale thanked him and said that he had been honoured enough already.

"I have seen tears in the eyes of an emperor, and that is a great enough treasure for me. There is a strange power in an emperor's tears and God knows that is reward enough." Then he sang yet another song.

"That was the most charming and elegant song we have ever heard," said all the ladies of the court. And from that time onward they filled their mouths with water, so they could make a clucking noise, whenever anyone spoke to them, because they thought that then they sounded like the nightingale. Even the chambermaids and the lackeys were satisfied; and that really meant something, for servants are the most difficult to please. Yes, the nightingale was a success.

He was to have his own cage at court, and permission to take a walk twice a day and once during the night. Twelve servants were to accompany him; each held on tightly to a silk ribbon that was attached to the poor bird's legs. There wasn't any pleasure in such an outing.

The whole town talked about the marvellous bird. Whenever two people met in the street they would sigh; one would say, "night," and the other, "gale"; and then they would understand each other perfectly. Twelve delicatessen shop owners named their children "Nightingale," but not one of them could sing.

One day a package arrived for the emperor; on it was written: "Nightingale."

"It is probably another book about our famous bird," said the emperor. But he was wrong; it was a mechanical nightingale. It lay in a little box and was supposed to look like the real one, though it was made of silver and gold and studded with sapphires, diamonds, and rubies. When you wound it up, it could sing one of the songs the real nightingale sang; and while it performed its little silver tail would go up and down. Around its neck hung a ribbon on which was written: "The Emperor of Japan's nightingale is inferior to the Emperor of China's."

"It is beautiful!" exclaimed the whole court. And the messenger who had brought it had the title of Supreme Imperial Nightingale Deliverer bestowed upon him at once.

"They ought to sing together, it will be a duet," said everyone, and they did. But that didn't work out well at all; for the real bird sang in his own manner and the mechanical one had a cylinder inside its chest instead of a heart. "It is not its fault," said the imperial music master. "It keeps perfect time, it belongs to my school of music." Then the mechanical nightingale had to sing solo. Everyone agreed that its song was just as beautiful as the real nightingale's; and besides, the artificial bird was much pleasanter to look at, with its sapphires, rubies, and diamonds that glittered like bracelets and brooches.

The mechanical nightingale sang its song thirty-three times and did not grow tired. The court would have liked to hear it the thirty-fourth time, but the emperor thought that the real nightingale ought to sing now. But where was it? Nobody had noticed that he had flown out through an open window, to his beloved green forest.

"What is the meaning of this!" said the emperor angrily, and the whole court blamed the nightingale and called him an ungrateful creature.

"But the best bird remains," they said, and the mechanical bird sang its song once more. It was the same song, for it knew no other; but it was very intricate, so the courtiers didn't know it by heart yet. The imperial music master praised the bird and declared that it was better than the real nightingale, not only on the outside where the diamonds were, but also inside.

"Your Imperial Majesty and gentlemen: you understand that the real nightingale cannot be depended upon. One never knows what he will sing; whereas, in the mechanical bird, everything is determined. There is one song and no other! One can explain everything. We can open it up to examine and appreciate how human thought has fashioned the wheels and the cylinder, and put them where they are, to turn just as they should."

"Precisely what I was thinking!" said the whole court in a chorus. And the imperial music master was given permission to show the new nightingale to the people on the following Sunday.

The emperor thought that they, too, should hear the bird. They did and they were as delighted as if they had got drunk on too much tea. It was all very Chinese. They pointed with their licking fingers toward heaven, nodded, and said: "Oh!"

But the poor fisherman, who had heard the real nightingale, mumbled, "It sounds beautiful and like the bird's song, but something is missing, though I don't know what it is."

The real nightingale was banished from the empire.

The mechanical bird was given a silk pillow to rest upon, close to the emperor's bed; and all the presents it had received were piled around it. Among them were both gold and precious stones. Its title was Supreme Imperial Night-table Singer and its rank was Number One to the Left. —The emperor thought the left side was more distinguished because that is the side where the heart is, even in an emperor.

The imperial music master wrote a work in twenty-five volumes about the mechanical nightingale. It was not only long and learned but filled with the most difficult Chinese words, so everyone bought it and said they had read and understood it, for otherwise they would have been considered stupid and had to have their stomachs poked.

A whole year went by. The emperor, the court, and all the Chinese in China knew every note of the supreme imperial night-table singer's song by heart; but that was the very reason why they liked it so much: they could sing it themselves, and they did. The street urchins sang: "Zi-zi-zizzi, cluck-cluck-cluck-cluck." And so did the emperor. Oh, it was delightful!

But one evening, when the bird was singing its very best and the emperor was lying in bed listening to it, something said: "Clang," inside it. It was broken! All the wheels whirred around and then the bird was still.

The emperor jumped out of bed and called his physician but he couldn't do anything, so the imperial watchmaker was fetched. After a great deal of talking and tinkering he repaired the bird, but he declared that the cylinders were worn and new ones could not be fitted. The bird would have to be spared; it could not be played so often.

It was a catastrophe. Only once a year was the mechanical bird allowed to sing, and then it had difficulty finishing its song. But the imperial music master made a speech wherein he explained, using the most difficult words, that the bird was as good as ever; and then it was.

Five years passed and a great misfortune happened. Although everyone loved the old emperor, he had fallen ill; and they all agreed that he would not get well again. It was said that a new emperor had already been chosen; and when people in the street asked the chief courtier how the emperor was, he would shake his head and say: "P."

Pale and cold, the emperor lay in his golden bed. The whole court believed him to be already dead and they were busy visiting and paying their respects to the new emperor. The lackeys were all out in the street gossiping, and the chambermaids were drinking coffee. All the floors in the whole palace were covered with black carpets so that no one's steps would disturb the dying emperor; and that's why it was as quiet as quiet could be in the whole palace.

But the emperor was not dead yet. Pale and motionless he lay in his great golden bed; the long velvet curtains were drawn, and the golden tassels moved slowly in the wind, for one of the windows was open. The moon shone down upon the emperor, and its light was reflected in the diamonds of the mechanical bird.

The emperor could hardly breathe; he felt as though someone were sitting on his chest. He opened his eyes. Death was sitting there. He was wearing the emperor's golden crown and held his gold sabre in one hand and his imperial banner in the other. From the folds of the curtains that hung around his bed, strange faces looked down at the emperor. Some of them were frighteningly ugly, and others mild and kind. They were the evil and good deeds that the emperor had done. Now, while Death was sitting on his heart, they were looking down at him.

"Do you remember?" whispered first one and then another. And they told him things that made the cold sweat of fear appear on his forehead.

"No, no, I don't remember! It is not true!" shouted the emperor. "Music, music, play the great Chinese gong," he begged, "so that I will not be able to hear what they are saying."

But the faces kept talking and Death, like a real Chinese, nodded his head to every word that was said.

"Little golden nightingale, sing!" demanded the emperor. "I have given you gold and precious jewels and with my own hands have I hung my golden slipper around your neck. Sing! Please sing!"

But the mechanical nightingale stood as still as ever, for there was no one to wind it up; and then, it couldn't sing.

Death kept staring at the emperor out of the empty sockets in his skull; and the palace was still, so terrifyingly still.

All at once the most beautiful song broke the silence. It was the nightingale, who had heard of the emperor's illness and torment. He sat on a branch outside his window and sang to bring him comfort and hope. As he sang, the faces in the folds of the curtains faded and the blood pulsed with greater force through the emperor's weak body. Death himself listened and said, "Please, little nightingale, sing on!"

"Will you give me the golden sabre? Will you give me the imperial banner? Will you give me the golden crown?"

Death gave each of his trophies for a song; and then the nightingale sang about the quiet churchyard, where white roses grow, where fragrant elderberry trees are, and where the grass is green from the tears of those who come to mourn. Death longed so much for his garden that he flew out of the window, like a white cold mist.

"Thank you, thank you," whispered the emperor, "you heavenly little bird, I remember you. You have I banished from my empire and yet you came to sing for me; and when you sang the evil phantoms that taunted me disappeared, and Death himself left my heart. How shall I reward you?"

"You have rewarded me already," said the nightingale. "I shall never forget that, the first time I sang for you, you gave me the tears from your eyes; and to a poet's heart, those are jewels. But sleep so you can become well and strong; I shall sing for you."

The little grey bird sang; and the emperor slept, so blessedly, so peacefully.

The sun was shining in through the window when he woke; he did not feel ill any more. None of his servants had come, for they thought that he was already dead; but the nightingale was still there and he was singing.

"You must come always," declared the emperor. "I shall only ask you to sing when you want to. And the mechanical bird I shall break in a thousand pieces."

"Don't do that," replied the nightingale. "The mechanical bird sang as well as it could, keep it. I can't build my nest in the palace; let me come to visit you when I want to, and I shall sit on the branch outside your window and sing for you. And my song shall make you happy and make you thoughtful. I shall sing not only of those who are happy but also of those who suffer. I shall sing of the good and of the evil that happen around you, and yet are hidden from you. For a little songbird flies far. I visit the poor fisherman's cottage and the peasant's hut, far away from your palace and your court. I love your heart more than your crown, and yet I feel that the crown has a fragrance of something holy about it. I will come! I will sing for you! Only one thing must you promise me."

"I will promise you anything," said the emperor, who had dressed himself in his imperial clothes and was holding his golden sabre, pressing it against his heart.

"I beg of you never tell anyone that you have a little bird that tells you everything, for then you will fare even better." And with those words the nightingale flew away.

The servants entered the room to look at their dead master. There they stood gaping when the emperor said: "Good morning."

The Princess and the Pea

Once upon a time there was a prince who wanted to marry a princess, but she would have to be a real one. He travelled around the whole world looking for her; but every time he met a princess there was always something amiss. There were plenty of princesses but not one of them was quite to his taste. Something was always the matter: they just weren't real princesses. So he returned home very sad and sorry, for he had set his heart on marrying a real princess.

One evening a storm broke over the kingdom. The lightning flashed, the thunder roared, and the rain came down in bucketfuls. In the midst of this horrible storm, someone knocked on the city gate; and the king himself went down to open it.

On the other side of the gate stood a princess. But goodness, how wet she was! Water ran down her hair and her clothes in streams. It flowed in through the heels of her shoes and out through the toes. But she said that she was a real princess.

"We'll find that out quickly enough," thought the old queen, but she didn't say a word out loud. She hurried to the guest room and took all the bedclothes off the bed; then on the bare bedstead she put a pea. On top of the pea she put twenty mattresses; and on top of the mattresses, twenty eiderdown quilts. That was the bed on which the princess had to sleep.

In the morning, when someone asked her how she had slept, she

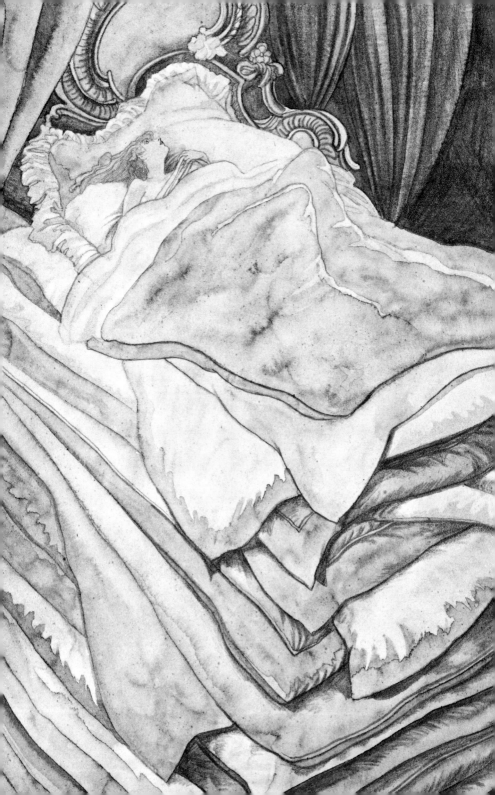

replied, "Oh, just wretchedly! I didn't close my eyes once, the whole night through. God knows what was in that bed; but it was something hard, and I am black and blue all over."

Now they knew that she was a real princess, since she had felt the pea that was lying on the bedstead through twenty mattresses and twenty eiderdown quilts. Only a real princess could be so sensitive!

The prince married her. The pea was exhibited in the royal museum; and you can go there and see it, if it hasn't been stolen.

Now that was a real story!

The Swineherd

There once was a poor prince. He had a kingdom and, though it wasn't very big, it was large enough to marry on, and married he wanted to be.

Now it was rather bold of him to say to the emperor's daughter: "Do you want me?" But he was a young man of spirit who was quite famous, and there were at least a hundred princesses who would have said thank you very much to his proposal. But the emperor's daughter didn't. Let me tell you the story.

On the grave of the prince's father there grew a rose tree. It was a beautiful tree that only flowered every fifth year; and then it bore only one rose. That rose had such a sweet fragrance that anyone who smelled it forgot immediately all his sorrow and troubles. The prince also owned a nightingale which sang as though all the melodies ever composed lived in its throat—so beautiful was its song. The prince decided to send the rose and the nightingale to the emperor's daughter, and had two little silver chests made to put them in.

The emperor ordered the gifts to be carried into the grand assembly room where the princess was playing house with her ladies in waiting. That was their favourite game and they never played any other. When the princess saw the pretty little silver chests she clapped her hands and jumped for joy.

"Oh, I hope one of them contains a pretty little kitten," she said; but when she opened the chest, she found a rose.

"It is very prettily made," said one of the ladies in waiting.

"It is more than pretty; it is nice," remarked the emperor. Then the princess touched the rose and she almost wept with disappointment.

"Oh, Papa," she shrieked. "It is not glass, it's real!"

"Oh, oh!" shrieked all the ladies in waiting. "How revolting! It is real!"

"Let's see what is in the other chest first, before we get angry," admonished the emperor. There was the nightingale, who sang so beautifully that it was difficult to find anything wrong with it.

"*Superbe! Charmant!*" said the ladies in waiting. They all spoke French, one worse than the other.

"That bird reminds me of the late empress' music box," said an old courtier. "It has the same tone, the same sense of rhythm."

"You are right," said the emperor, and cried like a baby.

"I would like to know if that is real too," demanded the princess.

"Oh yes, it is a real bird," said one of the pages who had brought the gifts.

"In that case we will let the bird fly away," said the princess; and she sent a messenger to say that she would not even permit the prince to come inside her father's kingdom.

But the prince was not easily discouraged. He smeared his face with both black and brown shoe polish, put a cap on his head, then he walked up to the emperor's castle and knocked.

"Good morning, Emperor," said the young man, for it was the emperor himself who had opened the door. "Can I get a job in the castle?"

"Oh, there are so many people who want to work here," answered the emperor, and shook his head. "But I do need someone to tend the pigs, we have such an awful lot of them."

And so the prince was hired as the emperor's swineherd. There was a tiny, dirty room next to the pigpen, and that was where he was expected to live.

The young man spent the rest of the day making a very pretty little pot. By evening it was finished. The pot had little bells all around it, and when it boiled, they played that old song:

> *Ach, du lieber Augustin,*
> *Alles ist weg, weg, weg.*

But the strangest and most wonderful thing about the pot was that, if you held your finger in the steam above it, then you could smell what was cooking on any stove in town. Now there was something a little different from the rose.

The princess was out walking with her ladies in waiting, and when she heard the musical pot she stopped immediately. She listened and smiled, for "Ach, du lieber Augustin" she knew. She could play the melody herself on the piano with one finger.

"It is a song I know!" she exclaimed. "That swineherd must be cultured. Please go in and ask him what the instrument costs."

One of the ladies in waiting was ordered to run over to the pigpen, but she put wooden shoes on first.

"What do you want for the pot?" she asked.

"Ten kisses from the princess," said the swineherd.

"God save us!" cried the lady in waiting.

"I won't settle for less," said the swineherd.

"Well, what did he want?" asked the princess.

"I can't say it," blushed the lady in waiting.

"Then you can whisper it," said the princess; and the lady in waiting whispered.

"He is very naughty," said the princess, and walked on. But she had gone only a few steps when she heard the little bells play again, and they sounded even sweeter to her than they had before.

> *Ach, du lieber Augustin,*
> *Alles ist weg, weg, weg.*

"Listen," she said, "ask him if he will be satisfied with ten kisses from one of my ladies in waiting."

"No, thank you!" replied the swineherd to that proposal. "Ten kisses from the princess or I keep my pot."

"This is most embarrassing," declared the princess. "You will all have to stand around me so no one can see it."

And the ladies in waiting formed a circle and held out their skirts so no one could peep. The swineherd got his kisses and the princess the pot.

Oh, what a grand time they had! All day and all evening they made the little pot boil. There wasn't a stove in the whole town that had anything cooking on it that they didn't know about. They knew what was served for dinner on every table: both the count's and the cowherd's. The ladies

in waiting were so delighted that they clapped their little hands.

"We know who is going to have soup and pancakes and who is eating porridge and rib roast! Oh, it is most interesting."

"Very!" said the imperial housekeeper.

"Keep your mouth shut. Remember, I am the princess," said the emperor's daughter.

And all the ladies in waiting and the imperial housekeeper said: "God preserve us, we won't say a word."

The swineherd — that is to say, the prince whom everyone thought was a swineherd — did not like to waste his time, so he constructed a rattle which was so ingenious that, when you swung it around, it played all the waltzes, polkas, and dance melodies ever composed since the creation of the world.

"It is superb!" exclaimed the princess as she was walking past the pigsty. "I have never heard a more exquisite composition. Do go in and ask what he wants for the instrument, but I won't kiss him!"

"He wants a hundred kisses from the princess," said the lady in waiting who had been sent to speak to the swineherd.

"He must be mad," declared the princess. She walked on a few steps and then she stood still. "One ought to encourage art," she said. "I am the emperor's daughter. Tell him he can have ten kisses from me just as he got yesterday. The rest he can get from my ladies in waiting."

"But we don't want to kiss him," they all cried.

"Stuff and nonsense!" replied the princess, for she was angry. "If I can kiss him, you can too. Besides, what do you think I give you room and board for?"

And one of the ladies in waiting went to talk with the swineherd. "One hundred kisses from the princess or I keep the rattle," was the message she came back with.

"Then gather around me!" commanded the princess. The ladies in waiting took their positions and the kissing began.

"I wonder what is going on down there by the pigsty," said the emperor, who was standing out on the balcony. He rubbed his eyes and put his glasses on. "It is the ladies in waiting. What devilment are they up to? I'd better go down and see." Then he pulled up the backs of his slippers, for they were really only a comfortable old pair of shoes with broken backs. Oh, how he ran! But as soon as he came near the pigsty he walked on tiptoe.

The ladies in waiting were so busy counting kisses—to make sure that the bargain was justly carried out and that the swineherd did not get one kiss too many or one too few—that they didn't hear or see the emperor, who was standing on tiptoe outside the circle.

"What's going on here?" he shouted. When he saw the kissing he took off one of his slippers and started hitting the ladies in waiting on the tops of their heads, just as the swineherd was getting his eighty-sixth kiss.

"*Heraus!* Get out!" he screamed, for he was really angry; and both the swineherd and the princess were thrown out of his empire.

There they stood: the princess was crying, the swineherd was grumbling, and the rain was streaming down.

"Oh, poor me!" wailed the princess. "If only I had married the prince. Oh, I am so unhappy!"

The swineherd stepped behind a tree, rubbed all the black and brown shoe polish off his face, and put on his splendid royal robes. He looked so impressive that the princess curtsied when saw him.

"I have come to despise you," said the prince. "You did not want an honest prince. You did not appreciate the rose or the nightingale, but you could kiss a swineherd for the sake of a toy. Farewell!"

The prince entered his own kingdom and locked the door behind him; and there the princess could stand and sing:

> "*Ach, du lieber Augustin,*
> *Alles ist weg, weg, weg.*"

For, indeed, everything was "all gone!"

The Ugly Duckling

It was so beautiful out in the country. It was summer. The oats were still green, but the wheat was turning yellow. Down in the meadow the grass had been cut and made into haystacks; and there the storks walked on their long red legs talking Egyptian, because that was the language they had been taught by their mothers. The fields were enclosed by woods, and hidden among them were little lakes and pools. Yes, it certainly was lovely out there in the country!

The old castle, with its deep moat surrounding it, lay bathed in sunshine. Between the heavy walls and the edge of the moat there was a narrow strip of land covered by a whole forest of burdock plants. Their leaves were large and some of the stalks were so tall that a child could stand upright under them and imagine that he was in the middle of the wild and lonely woods. Here a duck had built her nest. While she sat waiting for the eggs to hatch, she felt a little sorry for herself because it was taking so long and hardly anybody came to visit her. The other ducks preferred swimming in the moat to sitting under a dock leaf and gossiping.

Finally the eggs began to crack. "Peep . . . Peep," they said one after another. The egg yolks had become alive and were sticking out their heads.

"Quack . . . Quack . . . " said their mother. "Look around you." And the ducklings did; they glanced at the green world about them, and that was what their mother wanted them to do, for green was good for their eyes.

"How big the world is!" piped the little ones, for they had much more space to move around in now than they had had inside the egg.

"Do you think that this is the whole world?" quacked their mother. "The world is much larger than this. It stretches as far as the minister's wheat fields, though I have not been there . . . Are you all here?" The duck got up and turned around to look at her nest. "Oh no, the biggest egg hasn't hatched yet; and I'm so tired of sitting here! I wonder how long it will take?" she wailed, and sat down again.

"What's new?" asked an old duck who had come visiting.

"One of the eggs is taking so long," complained the mother duck. "It won't crack. But take a look at the others. They are the sweetest little ducklings you have ever seen; and every one of them looks exactly like their father. That scoundrel hasn't come to visit me once."

"Let me look at the egg that won't hatch," demanded the old duck. "I am sure that it's a turkey egg! I was fooled that way once. You can't imagine what it's like. Turkeys are afraid of the water. I couldn't get them to go into it. I quacked and I nipped them, but nothing helped. Let me see that egg! . . . Yes, it's a turkey egg. Just let it lie there. You go and teach your young ones how to swim, that's my advice."

"I have sat on it so long that I suppose I can sit a little longer, at least until they get the hay in," replied the mother duck.

"Suit yourself," said the older duck, and went on.

At last the big egg cracked too. "Peep . . . Peep," said the young one, and tumbled out. He was big and very ugly.

The mother duck looked at him. "He's awfully big for his age," she said. "He doesn't look like any of the others. I wonder if he could be a turkey? Well, we shall soon see. Into the water he will go, even if I have to kick him to make him do it."

The next day the weather was gloriously beautiful. The sun shone on the forest of burdock plants. The mother duck took her whole brood to the moat. "Quack . . . Quack . . . " she ordered.

One after another, the little ducklings plunged into the water. For a moment their heads disappeared, but then they popped up again and the little ones floated like so many corks. Their legs knew what to do without being told. All of the new brood swam very nicely, even the ugly one.

"He is no turkey," mumbled the mother. "See how beautifully he uses his legs and how straight he holds his neck. He is my own child and, when you look closely at him, he's quite handsome . . . Quack! Quack! Follow me and I'll take you to the henyard and introduce you to everyone. But stay close to me, so that no one steps on you, and look out for the cat."

They heard an awful noise when they arrived at the henyard. Two families of ducks had got into a fight over the head of an eel. Neither of them got it, for it was swiped by the cat.

"That is the way of the world," said the mother duck, and licked her bill. She would have liked to have had the eel's head herself. "Walk nicely," she admonished them. "And remember to bow to the old duck over there. She has Spanish blood in her veins and is the most aristocratic fowl here. That is why she is so fat and has a red rag tied around one of her legs. That is the highest mark of distinction a duck can be given. It means so much that she will never be done away with; and all the other fowl and the human beings know who she is. Quack! Quack! . . . Don't walk, waddle like well-brought-up ducklings. Keep your legs far apart, just as your mother and father have always done. Bow your heads and say, 'Quack!'" And that was what the little ducklings did.

Other ducks gathered about them and said loudly, "What do we want that gang here for? Aren't there enough of us already? Pooh! Look how ugly one of them is! He's the last straw!" And one of the ducks flew over and bit the ugly duckling on the neck.

"Leave him alone!" shouted the mother. "He hasn't done anyone any harm."

"He's big and he doesn't look like everybody else!" replied the duck who had bitten him. "And that's reason enough to beat him."

"Very good-looking children you have," remarked the duck with the red rag around one of her legs. "All of them are beautiful except one. He didn't turn out very well. I wish you could make him over again."

"That's not possible, Your Grace," answered the mother duck. "He may not be handsome, but he has a good character and swims as well as the others, if not a little better. Perhaps he will grow handsomer as he grows older and becomes a bit smaller. He was in the egg too long, and that is why he doesn't have the right shape." She smoothed his neck for a moment and then added, "Besides, he's a drake; and it doesn't matter so much what he looks like. He is strong and I am sure he will be able to take care of himself."

"Well, the others are nice," said the old duck. "Make yourself at home, and if you should find an eel's head, you may bring it to me."

And they were "at home."

The poor little duckling, who had been the last to hatch and was so ugly, was bitten and pushed and made fun of both by the hens and by the other ducks. The turkey cock (who had been born with spurs on, and therefore thought he was an emperor) rustled his feathers as if he were a full-rigged ship under sail, and strutted up to the duckling. He gobbled so loudly at him that his own face got all red.

The poor little duckling did not know where to turn. How he grieved over his own ugliness, and how sad he was! The poor creature was mocked and laughed at by the whole henyard.

That was the first day; and each day that followed was worse than the one before. The poor duckling was chased and mistreated by everyone, even his own sisters and brothers, who quacked again and again, "If only the cat would get you, you ugly thing!"

Even his mother said, "I wish you were far away." The other ducks bit him and the hens pecked at him. The little girl who came to feed the fowls kicked him.

At last the duckling ran away. He flew over the tops of the bushes, frightening all the little birds so that they flew up into the air. "They, too, think I am ugly," thought the duckling, and closed his eyes—but he kept on running.

Finally he came to a great swamp where wild ducks lived; and here he stayed for the night, for he was too tired to go any farther.

In the morning he was discovered by the wild ducks. They looked at him and one of them asked, "What kind of bird are you?"

The ugly duckling bowed in all directions, for he was trying to be as polite as he knew how.

"You are ugly," said the wild ducks, "but that is no concern of ours, as long as you don't try to marry into our family."

The poor duckling wasn't thinking of marriage. All he wanted was to be allowed to swim among the reeds and drink a little water when he was thirsty.

He spent two days in the swamp; then two wild geese came—or rather, two wild ganders, for they were males. They had been hatched not long ago; therefore they were both frank and bold.

"Listen, comrade," they said. "You are so ugly that we like you. Do you want to migrate with us? Not far from here there is a marsh where some beautiful wild geese live. They are all lovely maidens, and you are so ugly that you may seek your fortune among them. Come along."

"Bang! Bang!" Two shots were heard and both ganders fell down dead among the reeds, and the water turned red from their blood.

"Bang! Bang!" Again came the sound of shots, and a flock of wild geese flew up.

The whole swamp was surrounded by hunters; from every direction came the awful noise. Some of the hunters had hidden behind bushes or among the reeds but others, screened from sight by the leaves, sat on the long, low branches of the trees that stretched out over the swamp. The blue smoke from the guns lay like a fog over the water and among the trees. Dogs came splashing through the marsh, and they bent and broke the reeds.

The poor little duckling was terrified. He was about to tuck his head under his wing, in order to hide, when he saw a big dog peering at him through the reeds. The dog's tongue hung out of its mouth and its eyes glistened evilly. It bared its teeth. Splash! It turned away without touching the duckling.

"Oh, thank God!" he sighed. "I am so ugly that even the dog doesn't want to bite me."

The little duckling lay as still as he could while the shots whistled through the reeds. Not until the middle of the afternoon did the shooting stop; but the poor little duckling was still so frightened that he waited several hours longer before taking his head out from under his wing. Then he ran as quickly as he could out of the swamp. Across the fields and the meadows he went, but a wind had come up and he found it hard to make his way against it.

Towards evening he came upon a poor little hut. It was so wretchedly crooked that it looked as if it couldn't make up its mind which way to fall and that was why it was still standing. The wind was blowing so hard that the poor little duckling had to sit down in order not to be blown away. Suddenly he noticed that the door was off its hinges, making a crack; and he squeezed himself through it and was inside.

An old woman lived in the hut with her cat and her hen. The cat was called Sonny and could both arch his back and purr. Oh yes, it could also make sparks if you rubbed its fur the wrong way. The hen had very short legs and that was why she was called Cluck Lowlegs. But she was good at laying eggs, and the old woman loved her as if she were her own child.

In the morning the hen and the cat discovered the duckling. The cat meowed and the hen clucked.

"What is going on?" asked the old woman, and looked around. She couldn't see very well, and when she found the duckling she thought it was a fat, full-grown duck. "What a fine catch!" she exclaimed. "Now we shall have duck eggs, unless it's a drake. We'll give it a try."

So the duckling was allowed to stay for three weeks on probation, but he laid no eggs. The cat was the master of the house and the hen the mistress. They always referred to themselves as "we and the world," for they thought that they were half the world—and the better half at that. The duckling thought that he should be allowed to have a different opinion, but the hen did not agree.

"Can you lay eggs?" she demanded.

"No," answered the duckling.

"Then keep your mouth shut."

And the cat asked, "Can you arch your back? Can you purr? Can you make sparks?"

"No."

"Well, in that case, you have no right to have an opinion when sensible people are talking."

The duckling was sitting in a corner and was in a bad mood. Suddenly he recalled how lovely it could be outside in the fresh air when the sun shone: a great longing to be floating in the water came over the duckling, and he could not help talking about it.

"What is the matter with you?" asked the hen as soon as she had heard what he had to say. "You have nothing to do, that's why you get ideas like that. Lay eggs or purr, and such notions will disappear."

"You have no idea how delightful it is to float in the water, and to dive down to the bottom of a lake and get your head wet," said the duckling.

"Yes, that certainly does sound amusing," said the hen. "You must have gone mad. Ask the cat—he is the most intelligent being I know—ask him whether he likes to swim or dive down to the bottom of a lake. Don't take my word for anything. . . . Ask the old woman, who is the cleverest person in the world; ask her whether she likes to float and to get her head all wet."

"You don't understand me!" wailed the duckling.

"And if I don't understand you, who will? I hope you don't think that you are wiser than the cat or the old woman—not to mention myself.

Don't give yourself airs! Thank your Creator for all He has done for you. Aren't you sitting in a warm room, where you can hear intelligent conversation that you could learn something from? While you, yourself, do nothing but say a lot of nonsense and aren't the least bit amusing! Believe me, that's the truth, and I am only telling it to you for your own good. That's how you recognize a true friend: it's someone who is willing to tell you the truth, no matter how unpleasant it is. Now get to work: lay some eggs, or learn to purr and arch your back."

"I think I'll go out into the wide world," replied the duckling.

"Go right ahead!" said the hen.

And the duckling left. He found a lake where he could float in the water and dive to the bottom. There were other ducks, but they ignored him because he was so ugly.

Autumn came and the leaves turned yellow and brown, then they fell from the trees. The wind caught them and made them dance. The clouds were heavy with hail and snow. A raven sat on a fence and screeched, "Ach! Ach!" because it was so cold. When just thinking of how cold it was is enough to make one shiver, what a terrible time the duckling must have had.

One evening just as the sun was setting gloriously, a flock of beautiful birds came out from among the rushes. Their feathers were so white that they glistened; and they had long, graceful necks. They were swans. They made a very loud cry, then they spread their powerful wings. They were flying south to a warmer climate, where the lakes were not frozen in the winter. Higher and higher they circled. The ugly duckling turned round and round in the water like a wheel and stretched his neck up toward the sky; he felt a strange longing. He screeched so piercingly that he frightened himself.

Oh, he would never forget those beautiful birds, those happy birds. When they were out of sight the duckling dived down under the water to the bottom of the lake; and when he came up again he was beside himself. He did not know the name of those birds or where they were going, and yet he felt he loved them as he had never loved any other creatures. He did not envy them. It did not even occur to him to wish that he were so handsome himself. He would have been happy if the other ducks had let him stay in the henyard: that poor, ugly bird!

The weather grew colder and colder. The duckling had to swim round and round in the water, to keep just a little space for himself that wasn't frozen. Each night his hole became smaller and smaller. On all sides of him the ice creaked and groaned. The little duckling had to keep his feet constantly in motion so that the last bit of open water wouldn't become ice. At last he was too tired to swim any more. He sat still. The ice closed in around him and he was frozen fast.

Early the next morning a farmer saw him and with his clogs broke the ice to free the duckling. The man put the bird under his arm and took it home to his wife, who brought the duckling back to life.

The children wanted to play with him. But the duckling was afraid that they were going to hurt him, so he flapped his wings and flew right into the milk pail. From there he flew into a big bowl of butter and then into a barrel of flour. What a sight he was!

The farmer's wife yelled and chased him with a poker. The children laughed and almost fell on top of each other, trying to catch him; and how they screamed! Luckily for the duckling, the door was open. He got out of the house and found a hiding place beneath some bushes, in the newly fallen snow; and there he lay so still, as though there were hardly any life left in him.

It would be too horrible to tell of all the hardship and suffering the duckling experienced that long winter. It is enough to know that he did survive. When again the sun shone warmly and the larks began to sing, the duckling was lying among the reeds in the swamp. Spring had come!

He spread out his wings to fly. How strong and powerful they were! Before he knew it, he was far from the swamp and flying above a beautiful garden. The apple trees were blooming and the lilac bushes stretched their flower-covered branches over the water of a winding canal. Everything was so beautiful: so fresh and green. Out of a forest of rushes came three swans. They ruffled their feathers and floated so lightly on the water. The ugly duckling recognized the birds and felt again that strange sadness come over him.

"I shall fly over to them, those royal birds! And they can hack me to death because I, who am so ugly, dare to approach them! What difference does it make? It is better to be killed by them than to be bitten by the other ducks, and pecked by the hens, and kicked by the girl who tends the henyard; or to suffer through the winter."

And he lighted on the water and swam towards the magnificent swans. When they saw him they ruffled their feathers and started to swim in his direction. They were coming to meet him.

"Kill me," whispered the poor creature, and bent his head humbly while he waited for death. But what was that he saw in the water? It was his own reflection; and he was no longer an awkward, clumsy, grey bird, so ungainly and so ugly. He was a swan!

It does not matter that one has been born in the henyard as long as one has lain in a swan's egg.

He was thankful that he had known so much want, and gone through so much suffering, for it made him appreciate his present happiness and the loveliness of everything about him all the more. The swans made a circle around him and caressed him with their beaks.

Some children came out into the garden. They had brought bread with them to feed the swans. The youngest child shouted, "Look, there's a new one!" All the children joyfully clapped their hands, and they ran to tell their parents.

Cake and bread were cast on the water for the swans. Everyone agreed that the new swan was the most beautiful of them all. The older swans bowed towards him.

He felt so shy that he hid his head beneath his wing. He was too happy, but not proud, for a kind heart can never be proud. He thought of the time when he had been mocked and persecuted. And now everyone said that he was the most beautiful of the most beautiful birds. And the lilac bushes stretched their branches right down to the water for him. The sun shone so warm and brightly. He ruffled his feathers and raised his slender neck, while out of the joy in his heart, he thought, "Such happiness I did not dream of when I was the ugly duckling."

The Dung Beetle

The emperor's horse had been awarded golden shoes, one for each hoof. It was such a beautiful animal, with strong legs and a mane that fell like a veil of silk over its neck. Its eyes were sad, and when you looked into them you felt certain that if the horse could speak it would be able to answer more questions than you could ask. On the battlefield it had carried its master through a rain of bullets and a cloud of gun smoke. It was a true war horse, and once when the emperor was surrounded by the enemy, it had bit and kicked their horses and then, when all seemed lost, it had leaped over the carcass of an enemy steed to carry the emperor to safety. The horse had saved his master's golden crown and his life, which was worth a great deal more to the emperor than all the crown jewels. And that was why the blacksmith had been given orders to fasten a golden shoe on each of its hoofs.

The dung beetle climbed to the top of the manure pile to watch. "First the big and then the small," he said. "Not that size is important," he added as he lifted one of his thin legs and stretched it up toward the blacksmith.

"What do you want?" the man asked.

"Golden shoes," replied the dung beetle while balancing on five legs.

"You must be out of your mind to think that you should have golden shoes," the blacksmith exclaimed, and scratched himself behind his right ear.

"Golden shoes!" repeated the dung beetle crossly. "Am I not as good as that big clumsy beast that needs to have a servant to groom it, and even to see to it that it doesn't starve? Do I not belong to the emperor's stable too?"

"But why does the horse deserve golden shoes, have you any idea about that?"

"Idea!" cried the dung beetle. "I have a very good idea of how I deserve to be treated and how I am treated. Now I have been insulted enough; there is nothing left for me to do but go out into the wide world."

"Good riddance," said the smith.

"Brute!" returned the dung beetle, but the blacksmith, who had already returned to his work, did not hear him.

The dung beetle flew from the stable to the flower garden; it was a lovely place that smelled of roses and lavender.

"Isn't it beautiful here?" a ladybird called to him. She had just come for a visit and was busy folding her fragile wings beneath her black-spotted armour. "The flowers smell so sweet that I think I shall stay here forever."

The dung beetle sniffed. "I am used to something better. Why, there isn't even a decent pile of dung here."

The dung beetle sat down to rest in the shadow of a tiger lily. Climbing up the flower's stem was a caterpillar. "The world is beautiful," the caterpillar said. "The sun is very warm and I am getting quite sleepy. When I fall asleep—or die as some call it—I am sure that I shall wake up as a butterfly."

"Butterfly, indeed! Don't give yourself airs. I come from the emperor's stable, and no one there—not even the emperor's horse—has any notions like that. Those who can fly, fly. . . . And those who can crawl, crawl." And then the dung beetle flew away.

"I try not to let things annoy me; but they annoy me anyway," the dung beetle thought as it landed with a thud in the middle of a great lawn, where it lay quietly for a moment before falling asleep.

Goodness, it was raining. It poured! The dung beetle woke with a splash and tried to dig himself down into the earth but he couldn't. The rain had formed little rivers, and the dung beetle swam first on his stomach and then on his back. There was no hope of being able to fly. "I shan't live through it," he muttered, and sighed so deeply that his mouth filled with water. There was nothing to do but lie still where he was, and so he lay still.

When the rain let up for a moment the dung beetle blinked the water out of his eyes and looked about. He saw something white and crawled through the wet grass towards it. It was a piece of linen that had been stretched out on the grass to bleach. "I am used to better but it will have to do," he thought. "Though it's neither as warm nor as comfortable as a heap of dung; but when you travel you have to take things as they come."

And he stayed under the linen a whole day and a whole night; and it rained all the time. Finally, the following morning, the dung beetle stuck his head out from the fold of the linen and, seeing that the sky was grey, he was very annoyed.

Two frogs sat down on the linen. "What glorious weather," said one to the other. "It's so refreshing and this linen is soaking wet; to sit here is almost as pleasant as to swim."

"I would like to know,'" began the other frog, "if the swallow, who travels a good deal in foreign countries, ever has been in a land that has a better climate than ours. As much rain as you need; and a bit of wind, too—not to talk of the mist and the dew. Why, it is as good as living in a ditch. If you don't love this climate, then you don't love your country."

"Have you ever been in the emperor's stable?" the dung beetle asked. "There the wetness is spicy and warm. I prefer that kind of climate because I am used to it; but when you travel you can't take it with you, that's the way things are. . . . Could you tell me if there is a hothouse in this garden, where a person of my rank and sensitivity would feel at home?"

The frogs either couldn't or wouldn't understand him.

"I never ask a question more than once," said the dung beetle after he had repeated his query for the third time without getting an answer.

He walked along until he came upon a piece of a broken flowerpot. It shouldn't have been lying there but the gardener hadn't seen it, so it provided a good home for several families of earwigs. Earwigs do not need very much room, only company, especially lady earwigs, who are very motherly. Underneath the piece of pottery there lived several lady earwigs; and each of them thought that her children were the handsomest and most intelligent in the whole world.

"My son is engaged," one of them announced. "That innocent joy of my life. . . . His most cherished ambition is to climb into the ear of a minister. He is charmingly childish, and being engaged will keep him from running about, and that is a great comfort to a mother."

"Our son," began another mother earwig, "came straight out of the

egg. He is full of life and that is a joy. He is busy sowing his wild oats, and that, too, can make a mother proud. Don't you agree with me, Mr Dung Beetle?" She had recognized him by his shape.

"You are both right," remarked the dung beetle; and the earwigs invited him to come into their home and make himself comfortable.

"Now you must meet my children," said a third mother earwig.

"And mine!" cried a fourth. "They are so lovable and so amusing, and they only misbehave when they have stomach aches and it's not their fault that you get one so easily at their age."

All the mothers talked and their children talked; and when the little ones weren't talking, they were pulling at the dung beetle's moustache with the little tweezers that each of them had in his tail.

"Always up to something! Aren't they darling?" the mothers said in a chorus, and oozed mother love. But the dung beetle was bored and asked for directions to the nearest hothouse.

"It is far, far away, nearly at the end of the world, on the other side of the ditch," explained one of the lady earwigs. "If one of my children ever should think of travelling so far away I would die. I am sure of it."

"Well, that is where I am going," said the dung beetle, and to show that he was really gallant, he left without saying good-bye.

In the ditch he met many relatives: all of them dung beetles. "This is our home," they said. "It is quite comfortable: warm and wet. Please step down into the land of plenty. You must be tired after all your travels."

"I am!" replied the dung beetle. "I have lain a whole day and a whole night on linen. Cleanliness wears you out so. Then I stood under a draughty flowerpot until I got arthritis in my wings. It is a blessing to be with my own kind again."

"Do you come from the hothouse?" one of the older dung beetles asked.

"Higher still. I was born in the emperor's stable with golden shoes on. I am travelling incognito on a secret mission. And no matter how much you coaxed, I wouldn't tell you about it." With these words the dung beetle crept into the mud and made himself comfortable.

Nearby sat three young lady dung beetles. They were tittering because they didn't know what to say.

"They are not engaged, though they are beautiful," remarked their mother. The young ladies tittered again, this time because they were shy.

"Even in the emperor's stable I have never seen anyone more

beautiful," agreed the dung beetle, who had travelled far and wide.

"They are young and virtuous. Don't ruin them! Don't speak to them unless you have honourable intentions. But I see you are a gentleman, and therefore I give you my blessings!"

"Hurrah!" cried all the other dung beetles, and congratulated the foreigner on his engagement. First engaged, then married; there was no reason to put it off.

The first day of married life was good, and the second was pleasant enough, but on the third began all the responsibilities of providing food for his wives, and soon there would probably be offspring.

"They took me by surprise," thought the dung beetle. "Now I shall surprise them."

And so he did. He ran away. All day the wives waited, and all night too; then they declared themselves widows. The other dung beetles were angry and called him a ne'er-do-well, because they feared that now they would have to support the deserted wives.

"Just behave as if you were virgins again," said their mother. "Come, you are still my innocent girls. But shame on the tramp who abandoned you."

In the meantime, the dung beetle was sailing across the ditch on a cabbage leaf. It was morning and two human beings who happened to be passing noticed him and picked him up. They turned the dung beetle over and looked at him from all sides, for these two men were scholars.

The younger of the two, who was the most learned, said, " 'Allah sees the black scarab in the black stone that is part of the black mountain.' Isn't it written thus in the Koran?" Then he translated the dung beetle's name into Latin and gave a lecture in which he explained its genealogy and history. The older scholar remarked that there was no reason to take the dung beetle home with them, because he already had a much more beautiful scarab in his collection.

The dung beetle's feelings were hurt and he flew right out of the scholar's hand, high up into the sky. Now that his wings were dry he was able to make the long journey to the hothouse in one stretch. Luckily, a window was open and he flew straight in and landed on a pile of manure which had been delivered that morning.

"This is sumptuous," he said as he dug himself down into the dung, where he soon was asleep. He dreamed that the emperor' horse was dead and that he—the dung beetle—had not only been given its four golden shoes but had been promised two more. It was a pleasant dream and when the dung beetle awoke he climbed out of the manure to look about him. How magnificent everything was!

There were slender palm trees, whose green leaves appeared transparent when the sun shone on them; and below the trees were flowers of all colours. Some were red as fire, and some were yellow as amber, and some were as pure white as new-fallen snow. "What a marvellous display!" exclaimed the dung beetle. "And think how delicious it all will taste as soon as it is rotten. It is a glorious larder. I must go visiting and see if I can find any of my family living here. I cannot associate with just anybody. I have my pride, and that I am proud of." Then he crawled on, recalling as he did so, his dream and how the horse had died and he was given its gold shoes.

Suddenly a little hand picked him up, and again he was pinched and turned over. The gardener's son and one of his playmates had been exploring in the hothouse and, when they saw the dung beetle, they decided it would be fun to keep it. They wrapped it in a leaf from a grapevine, and the gardener's son stuck it in his pocket.

The dung beetle tried to creep and to crawl, and the boy closed his hand around him and that was most uncomfortable.

The boys ran to the big pond at the other end of the garden. A worn-out wooden shoe with a missing instep became a ship. With a stick for a mast and the dung beetle, who was tied to the stick with a piece of woollen thread, as the captain, the ship was launched.

The pool was large and the dung beetle thought he was adrift on an ocean. He got so frightened that he fell over on his back and there he lay with all his legs pointing up towards the sky.

There were currents in the water and they carried the wooden shoe along. When it got out too far, one of the boys would roll up his trousers—both boys were barefooted—and wade out to bring the shoe nearer the shore. Suddenly, while the shoe was quite far out, almost in the centre of the pond, someone called the boys, called them in so stern a voice that they forgot all about the shoe and ran home as fast as they could. The wooden shoe drifted on and on. The dung beetle shuddered with fear, for he couldn't fly away, tethered as he was to the mast.

A fly came to keep him company. "Lovely weather, don't you agree? I think I'll rest here for a moment in the sun. A very comfortable place you have here."

"Nonsense!" cried the dung beetle. "How can I be comfortable when I am tied to the mast? You talk like an idiot, so I'm sure you must be one."

"I'm not tied to anything," said the fly, and flew away.

"Now I know the world," muttered the dung beetle. "It is cruel and I am the only decent one in it. First they refused to give me golden shoes, then they made me lie on wet linen and stand for hours in a draught. Finally, I am tricked into marriage; and when I show my courage by going out into the world to find out what that's like and see how I will be treated there, I am captured by a human puppy who ties me to a mast and sets me adrift on a great ocean. And all the while the emperor's horse runs about with golden shoes on; and that's almost the most annoying part of it all. In this world you must not ask for sympathy. My life has been most interesting. . . . But what difference does that make if no one ever hears about it? . . . But does the world deserve to hear my story? . . . If it did, I would have been given the golden shoes. Had I got them, it would have brought honour to the stable. The stable missed its chance, so did the world, for everything is over."

But everything was not over; some young girls who were out rowing on the pond saw the little ship.

"Look, there is a wooden shoe," one of them said.

"Someone has tied a beetle to the mast," said another; and she leaned over the side of the boat and grabbed the wooden shoe. With a tiny pair of scissors she carefully cut the woollen thread, so that no harm came to the dung beetle. When they returned to shore the girl let him go in the grass. "Crawl or fly, whichever you can, for freedom is a precious gift," she said.

The dung beetle flew straight in through an open window of a large building and landed in the long, soft, silken mane of the emperor's horse, who was standing in the stable where they both belonged. He held on tightly to the mane, then he relaxed and began to think about life.

"Here I am, sitting on the emperor's horse. I am the rider. . . . What am I saying?" The dung beetle was talking out loud. "Now everything is clear to me! And I know it is true! Didn't the blacksmith ask me if I didn't have some idea why the emperor's horse was being shod with golden shoes? Now I understand that it was for my sake that the horse was given golden shoes."

The dung beetle was in the best of humours. "It is travelling that did it!" he thought. "It broadens your horizon and makes everything clear to you."

The sun shone through the window. Its rays fell upon the horse and the dung beetle. "The world is not so bad," remarked the dung beetle. "It all depends on how you look at it." And the world, indeed, was beautiful, when the emperor's horse was awarded golden shoes because the dung beetle was to ride it.

"I must dismount," he thought, "and go and tell the other dung beetles how I have been honoured. I will tell them of my wonderful adventures and how I enjoyed travelling abroad. And I'll tell them, too, that I have decided to stay at home until the horse wears out his golden shoes."

The Snowman

"It crackles and creaks inside of me. It is so cold that it is a pleasure," said the snowman. "When the wind bites you, then you know you're alive. Look how the burning one gapes and stares." By "the burning one" he meant the sun, which was just about to set. "But she can't make me blink; I'll stare right back at her."

The snowman had two triangular pieces of tile for eyes, and a children's rake for a mouth, which meant that he had teeth. His birth had been greeted by the boys with shouts of joy, to the sound of sleigh bells and the cracking of whips.

The sun set and the moon rose, full and round, beautiful in the blue evening sky.

"There she is again, just in another place. She couldn't stay away." The snowman thought that the sun had returned. "I suppose that I have cooled her off. But now she's welcome to stay up there, for it is pleasant with a bit of light, so that I can see. If only I knew how to move and get about, then I would go down to the lake and slide on the ice as the boys do. But I don't know how to run."

"Out! Out! Out!" barked the old watchdog, who was chained to his doghouse. He was hoarse and had been so ever since he had been refused entrance to the house. That was a long time ago now; but when the dog lived inside, he had lain next to the stove. "The sun will teach you to run. I

57

saw what happened to last year's snowman and to the one the year before last. . . . Out! Out! Out! . . . They are all gone."

"What do you mean by that, comrade?" asked the snowman. "How can that round one up there teach me to run?" By "that round one", he meant the moon. "She ran when I looked straight into her eyes. Now she is trying to sneak back from another direction."

"You are ignorant," said the watchdog. "But you have only just been put together. The round one up there is called the moon. The other one is the sun and she will be back tomorrow. She will teach you how to run, right down to the lake. I've got a pain in my left hind leg and that means the weather is about to change."

"I don't understand him," thought the snowman, "but I have a feeling that he was saying something unpleasant. The hot one—the one that was here a moment ago and then went away, the one he called the sun—is no friend of mine. Not that she's done me any harm; it's just a feeling I have."

The weather did change. In the morning there was a heavy fog. During the day it lifted, the wind started to blow, and there was frost. The sun came out and what a beautiful sight it was! The hoarfrost made the forest appear like a coral reef; every tree and bush looked as if it were decked with white flowers. In the summer when they have leaves, you cannot see what intricate and lovely patterns the branches make. But now they looked like lace and were so white that they seemed to radiate light. The weeping birch tree swayed in the wind as it did in summer. Oh, it was marvellous to see. As the sun rose higher in the sky its light grew sharper and its rays made everything appear as if it were covered with diamond dust. In the blanket of snow that lay upon the ground were large diamonds, blinking like a thousand small candles, whose light was whiter than snow.

"Isn't it unbelievably beautiful?" said a young girl who was taking a walk in the garden with a young man. "I think it's even lovelier now than it is in summer." And her eyes shone, as if the beauty of the garden were reflected in them.

They stopped near the snowman to admire the forest. "And a handsome fellow like that you won't see in the summer either," remarked the young man, pointing to the snowman.

The girl laughed and curtsied before the snowman, then she took the young man's hand in hers and the two of them danced across the snow, which crunched beneath their feet as if they were walking on grain.

"Who were they?" the snowman asked the dog. "You've been here on the farm longer than I have. Do you know them?"

"Certainly," answered the old dog. "She has patted me and he has given me bones. I would never bite either of them."

"Why do they walk hand in hand? I have never seen boys walk like that."

"They are engaged," the old dog sniffed. "Soon they will be moving into the same doghouse and will share each other's bones."

"Are they as important as you and I?" asked the snowman.

"They belong to the house and are our masters," replied the dog. "You certainly know precious little, even if you were only born yesterday. I wouldn't have believed such ignorance existed if I hadn't heard it with my own ears. But I have both age and knowledge, and from them you acquire wisdom. I know everyone on the farm; and I have known better times, when I didn't have to stand here, chained up and frozen to the bone. . . . Out! Out! Get out!"

"I love to freeze," said the snowman. "Tell me about the time when you were young, but stop rattling your chain like that, it makes me shudder inside."

"Out! Out!" barked the old dog. "I was a puppy once. 'See that lovely little fellow,' they used to say, and I slept on a velvet chair. I lay in the lap of the master of the house and had my paws wiped with embroidered handkerchiefs. They kissed me and called me a sweetheart, and their little doggy-woggy. When I grew too big to lie in a lap they gave me to the housekeeper. She had a room in the cellar. You can look right into her window from where you are standing. Down there I was the master. It wasn't as nicely furnished as upstairs, but it was much more comfortable. I had my own pillow to lie on, and the housekeeper gave me just as good food and more of it. Besides, upstairs there were children and they are a plague, always picking you up, squeezing you, and hugging you, and carrying you about as if you had no legs of your own to walk on. . . . Then there was the stove. In winter there is nothing as lovely as a stove. When it was really cold I used to crawl all the way under it. I still dream of being there, though it's a long time since I was there last. . . . Out! Out! Out!"

"Is a stove a thing of beauty?" asked the snowman. "Does it look like me?"

"You're as much alike as day and night. The stove's as black as coal; it has a long black neck with a brass collar around it. The fire's in the bottom. The stove lives on wood, which it eats so fast that it breathes fire out of its mouth. Ah! To lie near it or, better still, underneath it; until you have tried that you have no idea what comfort is. . . . You must be able to see it from where you are. That window, there, just look in."

And the snowman did and he saw the stove: a black, polished metal figure with brass fixtures. The little door at the bottom, through which ashes could be removed, had a window in it; and the snowman could see the light from the fire. A strange feeling of sadness and joy came over him. A feeling he had never experienced before. A feeling that all human beings know, except those who are made of snow.

"Why did you leave her?" The snowman somehow felt certain that the stove was of the female sex. "How could you bear to go away from such a lovely place?"

"I had to," answered the old watchdog. "They threw me out, put a chain around my neck, and here I am. And all I had done was to bite the youngest of the children from upstairs. I was gnawing on a bone and he took it away. A bone for a bone, I thought, and bit him in the leg. But the master and the mistress put all the blame on me. And ever since then I have been chained. The dampness has spoiled my voice. Can't you hear how hoarse I am? . . . Out! Out! Get out! . . . And that is the end of my story."

The snowman, who had stopped listening to the watchdog, was staring with longing through the cellar window into the housekeeper's room, where the stove stood on its four black legs. "She is exactly the same height as I am," he thought.

"It creaks so strangely inside me," the snowman muttered. "Shall I never be able to go down into the cellar and be in the same room with her? Isn't it an innocent wish, and shouldn't wishes be granted? It is my greatest, my most earnest, my only wish! And it would be a terrible injustice if it were never fulfilled! I shall get in, even if I have to break the window to do it."

"You will never get down into the cellar," the old dog said. "And if you did manage it, then the stove would make sure that you were out in a minute. . . . Out! Out!"

"I am almost out already!" cried the snowman. "I feel as if I were about to break in two."

All day long the snowman gazed through the window. In the evening the housekeeper's room seemed even more inviting. The light from the stove was so soft. It was not like the moonlight or the sunlight. "Only a

stove can glow like that," he thought. Every so often, when the top door of the stove was opened to put more wood in, the bright flames would shoot out, and the blaze would reflect through the window and make the snowman blush from the neck up.

"It's more than I can bear!" he exclaimed. "See how beautiful she is when she sticks out her tongue."

The night was long, but not for the snowman, who was daydreaming happily. Besides, it was so cold that everything seemed to tingle.

In the morning the cellar window was frozen; the most beautiful white flowers decorated the glass, which the snowman did not appreciate because they hid the stove from his view. It was so cold that the windows couldn't thaw and the running nose on the water pump in the yard grew an icicle. It was just the kind of weather to put a snowman in the best of moods, but it didn't. Why, it was almost a duty to be content with weather like that; but he wasn't. He was miserable. He was suffering from "stove-yearning".

"That is a very serious disease, especially for a snowman to get." The old watchdog shook his head. "I have suffered from it myself, but I got over it. . . . Out! Out! Get out! . . . I have a feeling that the weather is going to change."

And it did. It became warmer and the snowman became smaller. He didn't say a word, not even one of complaint, and that's a very telling sign.

One morning he fell apart. His head rolled off and something that looked like the handle of a broom stuck up from where he had stood. It was what the boys had used to help hold the snowman together and make him stand upright.

"Now I understand why he longed for the stove," said the old watchdog. "That's the old poker he had inside him. No wonder. Well, now that's over. . . . Out! Out! Out!"

And soon the winter was over, and the little girls sang:

> *"Come, anemones, so pure and white,*
> *Come, pussy willows, so soft and light,*
> *Come, lark and cuckoo, and sing*
> *That in February we have spring."*

And no one thought about the snowman.

The Snow Queen

A fairy tale told in seven stories

THE FIRST STORY, WHICH CONCERNS ITSELF WITH A BROKEN
MIRROR AND WHAT HAPPENED TO ITS FRAGMENTS

Listen! It's time to begin; and when we come to the end, we shall know more than we do now.

Once upon a time there was a troll, one of the most evil of them all: it was the devil! One day he was particularly pleased with himself because he had invented a mirror that had the power to make everything good and beautiful which it reflected appear so small that it was hardly there at all; while all that was worthless and ugly became more distinct and much more horrible. The loveliest landscape resembled cooked spinach. The kindest people looked repulsive or ridiculous. They might appear standing on their heads without any stomachs; their faces so distorted that no one could recognize them, for the tiniest freckle would spread out till it covered half a nose or a whole cheek, of that you could be sure.

"It's a very amusing mirror," said the devil. But the most amusing part of it all was that if a good or a kind thought passed through anyone's mind the most horrible grin would appear on the face in the mirror.

It was so entertaining that the devil himself laughed out loud. All the little trolls who went to troll school, where the devil was headmaster, said that a miracle had taken place. Now for the first time one could see what humanity and the world really looked like—at least, so they thought. They ran all over with the mirror, until there wasn't a place or a person in the whole world that had not been reflected and distorted in it.

At last they decided to fly up to heaven to poke fun at the angels and God Himself. All together they carried the mirror, and flew up higher and higher. The nearer they came to heaven, the harder the mirror laughed, so that the trolls could hardly hold on to it; still, they flew higher and higher: upward towards God and the angels, then the mirror shook so violently from laughter that they lost their grasp; it fell and broke into hundreds of millions of billions and some odd pieces. It was then that it really caused trouble, much more than it ever had before. Some of the splinters were as tiny as grains of sand and just as light, so that they were spread by the winds all over the world. When a sliver like that entered someone's eye it stayed there; and the person, forever after, would see the world distorted, and only be able to see the faults, and not the virtues, of everyone around him, since even the tinest fragment contained all the evil qualities of the whole mirror. If a splinter should enter someone's heart—oh, that was the most terrible of all!—that heart would turn to ice.

Some of the pieces of the mirror were so large that windowpanes could be made of them, although through such a window it was no pleasure to contemplate your friends. Some of the medium-sized pieces became spectacles—but just think of what would happen when you put on such a pair of glasses in order to see better and be able to judge more fairly. That made the devil laugh so hard that it tickled in his stomach, which he found very pleasant.

Some of the tinest bits of the mirror are still flying about in the air. And now you shall hear about them.

THE SECOND STORY, WHICH IS ABOUT A LITTLE BOY AND A
LITTLE GIRL

In a big city, where there live so many people and are so many houses that not every family can have a garden of their own and so must learn to be satisfied with a potted plant, there once lived a poor little girl and a poor little boy who had a garden a little bit larger than a flowerpot. They weren't brother and sister but loved each other as much as if they had been. They lived right across from each other; each family had a little apartment in the garret, but the houses were built so close together that the roofs almost touched. Between the two gutters that hung from the eaves and collected the water when it rained, there was only a very narrow space, and the two families could visit each other by climbing from one gable window to the other.

In front of the windows each family had a wooden box filled with earth, where herbs and other useful plants grew; but in each box there was also a little rose tree. The parents got the idea that, instead of setting the boxes parallel to their windows, they could set them across, so they reached from one window to the other. In that manner, the two gables were connected by a little garden. The peas climbed over the sides and hung down; and the little rose trees grew as tall as the windows and joined together, so that they looked like a green triumphal arch. The sides of the boxes were quite high and since the children could be relied upon not to try to climb over them, they were allowed to take their little wooden stools outside and sit under the rose trees; and there it was pleasant to play.

In winter that was not possible; the windows were tightly closed and sometimes they would be covered by ice. Then the little children would heat copper coins on the stove and press them against the glass until the roundest of holes would melt in the ice; through each of these peeped the loveliest little eye: one belonged to a little boy and the other to a little girl. His name was Kai and hers was Gerda. In summer they had to take only a few steps to be together; but in the winter they had to run up and down many stairs and across a yard covered by snowdrifts.

"The white bees are swarming," said Gerda's Grandmother.

"Do they have a queen too?" asked Kai, for he knew that real bees have such a ruler.

"Yes, they have," said the old woman. "She always flies right in the centre of the swarm, where the most snowflakes are. She is the biggest of them all, but she never lies down to rest as the other snowflakes do. No, when the wind dies she returns to the black clouds. Many a winter night she flies through the streets of the town and looks in through the windows; then they become covered by ice flowers."

"Yes, I've seen that!" said first one child and then the other; and now they knew that what Grandmother told them was true.

"Could the Snow Queen come inside, right into our room?" asked the little girl.

"Let her come," said Kai. "I will put her right on top of the stove and then she will melt."

Gerda's Grandmother patted his head and told them another story. But that night, as Kai was getting undressed in his own home, he climbed up on the chair by the window and looked out through his peephole. It was snowing gently; one of the flakes fell on the edge of the wooden box and stayed there; other snowflakes followed and they grew until they took the shape of a woman. Her clothes looked like the whitest gauze. It was made of millions of little star-shaped snowflakes. She was beautiful but all made of ice: cold, blindingly gittering ice; and yet she was alive, for her eyes stared at Kai like two stars, but neither rest nor peace was to be found in her gaze. She nodded toward the window and beckoned. The little boy got so frightened that he jumped down from the chair; and at that moment a shadow crossed the window as if a big bird had flown by.

The next day there was frost; but by noon the weather changed and it thawed. Soon it was spring again and the world grew green; the swallows returned to build their nests and the windows were opened. The little children sat in their garden, high above the other stories of the houses.

The roses bloomed marvellously that year. Gerda had just learned a psalm in which Our Saviour was compared to a rose. Her own roses reminded her of it. She sang and Kai joined her:

> *"Seek with the humble and the meek,*
> *In the dust for Our Saviour weep,*
> *In the valleys the roses grow*
> *There Child Jesus you shall know."*

Gerda and Kai held each other's hands, kissed the flowers, and looking up into God's bright sunshine, they spoke to it, as if the Child Jesus were there. Oh, those were lovely summer days, and it was glorious to sit under the little rose trees that seemed never to stop flowering.

One afternoon as Kai and Gerda sat looking at a picture book with animals and flowers in it—it was exactly five o'clock, for the bells in the church tower had just struck the hour—Kai said, "Ouch, ouch! Something pricked my heart!" And then again, "Ouch, something sharp is in my eye."

The little girl put her arms around his neck and looked into his eyes but there was nothing to be seen. Still, it hurt and little Gerda cried out of sympathy.

"I think it is gone now." said Kai. But he was wrong, two of the splinters from the devil's mirror had hit him: one had entered his heart and the other his eyes. You remember the mirror, it was that horrible invention of the devil which made everything good and decent look small and ridiculous, and everything evil and foul appear larger and more distinct. Poor Kai, soon his heart would turn to ice and his eyes would see nothing but faults in everything. But the pain, that would disappear.

"Why are you crying?" he demanded. "You look ugly when you cry. There is nothing the matter with me. Look!" he shouted. "That rose up there has been gnawed by a worm; and look at that one, it is all crooked. They are ugly roses, as ugly as the thing they are growing in." Then he kicked the sides of the box and tore off the two roses.

"What are you doing, Kai?" cried the little girl, and when Kai saw how frightened she was, he tore off yet another flower; and then climbed through the window into his parents' apartment, leaving Gerda to sit out there all alone.

Later, when she came to see him with her picture book, he told her that picture books were for babies. And when Grandmother told stories he would argue with her or—which was much worse—stand behind her chair with a pair of glasses on his nose and imitate her most cruelly. He did it so accurately that people laughed. Soon he learned to mimic everyone in the whole street. He had a good eye for their little peculiarities and knew how to copy them.

Everyone said, "That boy has his head screwed on right!" But it was the splinters of glass that were in his eyes and his heart that made him behave that way; that, too, was why he teased little Gerda all the time—she who loved him with all her heart.

He did not play as he used to; now his games were more grown up. One winter day when it was snowing he brought a magnifying glass and looked at the snowflakes that were falling on his blue coat.

"Look through the glass, Gerda," he said to his little playmate; and she did. Through the magnifying glass each snowflake appeared like a flower or ten-pointed star. They were, indeed, beautiful to see.

"Aren't they marvellous?" asked Kai. "And each of them is quite perfect; they are much nicer than real flowers. They are all flawless as long as they don't melt."

A little bit later he came by, with his sled on his back, and wearing his hat and woollen gloves. He screamed into Gerda's ear as loud as he could, "I have been allowed to go down to the big square and play with the other boys!" And away he went.

Now down in the snow-covered square the most daring of the boys would tie their sleds behind the farmers' wagons. It was good fun and they would get a good ride. While they were playing, a big white sled drove into the square; the driver was clad in a white fur coat and a white fur hat. The sled circled the square twice and Kai managed to attach his little sled on to the back of the big one. He wanted to hitch a ride.

Away he went; the sled turned the corner and was out of the square. It began to go faster and faster, and Kai wanted to untie his sled, but every time he was about to do it, the driver of the big white sled turned and nodded so kindly to him that he didn't. It was as if they knew each other. Soon they were past the city gate; and the snow was falling so heavily that Kai could not see anything. He untied the rope but it made no difference, his little sled moved on as if it were tied to the big one by magic. They travelled along with the speed of the wind. Kai cried out in fear but no one heard him. The snow flew around him. Every so often his sled leapt over something — a ditch or a fence — and he had to hold on with all his might. Kai was terrified. He wanted to say the Lord's Prayer but all he could remember were his multiplication tables.

The snowflakes grew bigger and bigger until they looked like white hens that were running alongside him. At last the big sled stopped and its driver stood up and turned around to look at Kai. The fur hat and the coat were made of snow; the driver was a woman: how tall and straight she stood. It was the Snow Queen!

"We have come far," she said. "You look cold. Come, creep inside my bearskin coat."

Kai got up from his own sled and walked over to the big one, where he sat down next to the Snow Queen. She put her fur coat around him, and it felt as if he lay down in a deep snowdrift.

"Are you still cold?" she asked, and kissed his forehead. Her kiss was colder than ice. It went right to his heart, which was already half made of ice. He felt as though he were about to die, but it hurt only for a minute, then it was over. Now he seemed stronger and he no longer felt how cold the air was.

"My sled, my sled, don't forget it!" he cried. And one of the white hens put it on her back and flew behind them. The Snow Queen kissed Kai once more, and then all memory of Gerda, her Grandmother, and his home disappeared.

"I shan't give you any more kisses," she said, "or I might kiss you to death."

Kai looked at the Snow Queen; he could not imagine that anyone could have a wiser or a more beautiful face; and she no longer seemed to be made of ice, as she had when he first saw her outside his window, the time she had beckoned to him. In his eyes she now seemed utterly perfect, nor did he feel any fear. He told her that he knew his multiplication tables, could figure in fractions, and knew by heart the population and area in square miles of every country in Europe.

The Snow Queen smiled, and somehow Kai felt that he did not know enough. He looked out into the great void of the night, for by now they were flying high up in the clouds, above the earth. The storm swept on and sang its old, eternal songs. Above oceans, forests, and lakes they flew; and the cold winter wind whipped the landscape below them. Kai heard the cry of the wolves and the hoarse voice of the crows. The moon came out, and into its large and clear disk Kai stared all through the long winter night. When daytime came he fell asleep at the feet of the Snow Queen.

THE THIRD STORY: THE FLOWER GARDEN OF THE OLD WOMAN WHO KNEW MAGIC

But how did little Gerda feel when Kai did not return? She asked everyone where he had gone and none could answer. The boys who had been in the square could only tell that they had seen him tie his little sled to the back of a big white sled that had driven out of the city gate.

No one knew where he had gone and little Gerda cried long and bitterly. As time passed people began to say that he must have died; probably he had drowned in the deep, dark river that ran close to the city. It was a long and dismal winter.

Finally spring came with warm sunshine.

"Kai is dead and gone!" sighed little Gerda.

"I don't believe that," said the sunbeams.

"No, he is dead and gone," she repeated, and asked the swallows if that were not true.

"We don't believe it," they answered.

At last little Gerda did not believe it either.

"I will put on my new red shoes, the ones Kai has never seen," she said one day. "And then I will go down to the river and ask it a few questions."

It was very early in the morning; she kissed her Grandmother, who was still asleep, put on her new red shoes, and walked out through the city gate and down to the river.

"Is it true that you have taken my playmate? I will give you my new red shoes if you will give him back to me."

She thought that the little waves nodded strangely; so she took her treasure, her new red shoes, and threw them out into the river. They struck the water not far from shore, and the little waves carried them back to her. It was as if the river did not want the shoes since it had not taken Kai. But little Gerda thought it was because she had not thrown the shoes out far enough; therefore, when she saw a rowing boat among the reeds, she climbed into it, and standing in the stern threw the shoes in the water again. Suddenly the boat began to move! It hadn't been moored and without realizing it, she had set it adrift. She turned around, prepared to leap to the shore, but it was already several yards away.

The boat floated faster and faster downstream. Poor Gerda was so frightened that she just sat down and cried. No one heard her except the swallows, and they could not carry her to land. But to comfort her, they flew alongside the boat, twittering: "We are here! We are here!".

Gerda sat perfectly still. She was in her stockinged feet; although her shoes were following the boat, they were far behind. The landscape was beautiful. On both sides of the river, beyond the flower-covered banks, there were meadows, where sheep and cows grazed. But there was not a human being to be seen.

"Maybe the river will carry me to Kai," Gerda thought. And that thought was a great comfort and she felt much happier.

On and on the boat drifted, and for hours she sat watching the green shores; then she saw a cherry orchard. In the middle of it stood a little house with windows of coloured glass and a straw roof. Before the door two wooden soldiers stood guard; they presented arms.

Little Gerda, thinking that they were alive, waved and called; but naturally, they did not answer. The current was carrying the boat towards the shore and Gerda started to shout for help, louder and louder.

An old lady appeared at the door of the house. She was wearing a broad-brimmed hat, on which had been painted the most lovely flowers. "Poor little child!" she cried when she saw Gerda. "What are you doing out there on the river by yourself? Why have you sailed out into the wide world all alone?" And as she spoke, she caught hold of the boat with her shepherd's crook and drew it into shore.

She lifted Gerda out of the boat. How happy the poor child was to be on dry land! But she was a little afraid of the old lady.

"Tell me who you are and how you got into such a predicament?" the old lady asked.

All the things that had happened to her, Gerda told the old lady; and when she finished she asked whether she had seen little Kai.

The old lady shook her head. "He hasn't passed my house," she replied. "But he will probably arrive here sooner or later. You mustn't be sad. Come and eat some of my cherries and look at my flowers. They are prettier than any picture book, and every one of them can tell a story." Taking Gerda by the hand, she led her into the house, and quickly closed the door.

There was a strange light in the room. The windows were placed very high up and the panes were of yellow, red, and blue glass. On the table stood a large bowl of cherries; they looked delicious, and Gerda ate as many as she could. While she was eating, the old lady was combing the child's hair with a golden comb. Oh, how prettily it curled around her beautiful rosebud face.

"I have longed so much for a little girl like you," she said. "You will see what good friends we shall become."

While her hair was being combed, Gerda began to forget about Kai. The old lady knew witchcraft; but she was not evil, she just liked to do a little magic for her own pleasure. And now more than anything else, she wanted little Gerda to stay with her. That was why she went out into her garden with her shepherd's crook, and pointed at all the roses. Immediately the sweet-smelling flowering bushes sank into the earth. They disappeared without a trace; and no one could even see where they had once stood. Now she need not fear that roses would make little Gerda think of little Kai and run away.

"Let me show you my garden," she said, leading Gerda by the hand.

Oh, what a beautiful place it was! All the flowers imaginable were there; and all of them in full bloom, although they belonged to different seasons. Certainly, no picture book could be as interesting and as lovely as they were. Gerda jumped for joy! She played with the flowers until the sun set behind the tall cherry trees. Then she was given the loveliest of beds, with a red quilt stuffed with dried violets; and there she slept, dreaming sweeter dreams than a queen on her wedding night.

The next morning, she went out again and played in the warm sunshine with the flowers; and in this manner, many days passed. Gerda knew every flower in the garden; and though there were so many different kinds, it seemed to her that there was one missing.

One afternoon, she found herself staring at the old lady's sun hat, with the painted flowers on its brim; and she noticed that the most beautiful among them was a rose. The old woman had forgotten the one in her hat, when she had got rid of all the roses—that happens, if you are absent-minded.

"What!" exclaimed Gerda. "Are there no roses in the garden?"

She looked everywhere, among all the flowers. She ran from one end of the garden to the other; but she did not find a rose. She felt so sad that she wept, and her tears fell on the very spot where a rose tree had grown. Through the earth, moistened by her tears, it shot up again, blooming just as beautifully as it had when the old woman made it vanish. Gerda kissed the flowers and thought of the roses at home and of little Kai.

"I have stayed here much too long," she cried. "I must find little Kai. Do you know where he is?" she asked the roses. "Do you think that he is dead?"

"No, he is not dead," answered the roses. "We have been down under the earth, where the dead are, and Kai was not there."

"Thank you," said little Gerda. She asked the other flowers if they knew where Kai was.

Every flower stood in the warm sunshine and dreamed its own fairy tale; and that it was willing to tell, but none of them knew anything about Kai.

What story did the tiger lily tell her? Here it is:

"Can you hear the drum: boom . . . boom! It has only two beats: boom . . . boom. Listen to the woman's song of lament; hear the priest chant. The Hindu wife is standing on the funeral pyre, dressed in a long red gown. Soon the flames will devour her and her husband's body. She is thinking of someone who is standing among the mourners; his eyes burn even hotter than the flames that lick her feet, his flaming eyes did burn her heart with greater heat than those flames which soon will turn her body into ashes. Can the fire of a funeral pyre extinguish the flame that burns within the heart?"

"That story I don't understand," said little Gerda.

"Well, it is my fairy tale," answered the tiger lily.

Next Gerda asked the honeysuckle; and this is what it said:

"High up above the narrow mountain road the old castle clings to the steep mountainside. Its ancient walls are covered by green ivy; the vines spread over the balcony where a beautiful young girl stands. No unplucked rose is fresher than she, no apple blossom, plucked and carried by the spring wind, is lighter or dances more daintily than she. Hear how her silk dress rustles. Will he not come soon?"

"Is that Kai you mean?" asked little Gerda.

"I tell only my own story, my own dream," answered the honeysuckle.

Now it was the little daisy's turn:

"Between two trees a swing has been hung. Two sweet little girls, with dresses as white as snow and from whose hats green ribbons hang, lazily swing back and forth. Their brother, who is older than they are, is standing up behind them on the swing. He has his arms around the ropes so that he will not fall. In one hand he has a little bowl; in the other, a clay pipe. He is blowing soap bubbles. The swing glides, and the bubbles with their ever changing colours fly through the air. The last bubble clings to the pipe, then the breeze takes it. A little black dog, which belongs to the children, stands on its hind legs barking at the bubble and it breaks. Such is my song: a swing and a world of foam."

"Your tale may be beautiful but you tell it so sadly, and you didn't mention Kai at all," complained little Gerda. "I think I will ask the hyacinth."

"There were three beautiful sisters; they were so fine and delicate that they were almost transparent. One had on a red dress; the second, a blue; and the third, a white one. They danced, hand in hand, down by the lake; but they were not elves, they were real human children. The air smelled so sweet that the girls wandered into the forest. The sweet fragrance grew stronger. Three coffins appeared; and in them lay the three beautiful sisters. They sailed across the lake, and glow-worms flew through the air like little candles. Were the dancing girls asleep or were they dead? The smell of the flowers said they were corpses, the bells at vespers ring for the dead."

"Oh, you make me feel so sad," said little Gerda. "And the fragrance from your flowers is so strong that it makes me think of the poor dead girls. Is Kai dead too? The roses, who have been down under the earth, said that he wasn't."

"Ding! dong!" rang the little hyacinth bells. "We are not tolling for Kai, we do not know him. We are singing our own little song, the only one we know."

Gerda approached a little buttercup that shone so prettily between its green leaves.

"You little sun, tell me, do you know where my playmate is?" she asked.

The buttercup's little shining face looked so trustfully back at her, but it too had only its own song to sing and it was not about Kai.

"Into a little narrow yard," began the buttercup, "God's warm sun was shining; it was the first spring day of the year. The sunbeams reflected against the white walls of the neighbour's house: nearby the first little yellow flower had unfolded itself. It was golden in the sunlight; the old grandmother brought her chair outside to sit in the warm sun. Her grandchild, the poor little servant maid, had come home for a short visit. She kissed her grandmother. There was gold in that kiss: the gold of the heart. Gold in the mouth, gold on the ground, and gold in the blessed sunrise. Now that was my little story," said the buttercup.

"Oh, my poor Grandmother," sighed little Gerda. "She must be longing for me and grieving, as she did when little Kai disappeared. But I will soon go back home and bring little Kai with me. There is no point in asking any of the other flowers, each one only sings its own song."

She tied her long dress up so that she could run fast, and away she went. The narcissus hit her leg smartly when she jumped over it and Gerda stopped. "What, do you know something?" she asked, and bent down toward the flower.

"I can see myself, I can see myself," cried the narcissus. "High up in the garret lives the little ballerina; she stands on tiptoe and kicks at the world, for it is but a mirage. She pours a little water from the kettle on a piece of cloth; it is her corset that she is washing, for cleanliness is next to godliness. Her white dress is hanging in the corner; it has also been washed in the tea-kettle, then it was hung out on the roof to dry. Now she puts it on, and around her neck she ties a saffron-coloured kerchief; it makes the dress seem even whiter. She lifts one leg high in the air. She is bending her stem.

I can see myself! I can see myself!"

"I don't care either to see you or to hear about you," said Gerda angrily. "Your story is a silly story," and with those words she ran to the other end of the garden.

The door in the wall was closed; she turned the old rusty handle and it sprang open. Out went little Gerda, in her bare feet, out into the wide world. Three times she looked back but no one was following her.

When she could not run any further, she sat down on a stone to rest. She noticed the landscape: summer was long since over, it was late autumn. Back in the old lady's garden time stood still, for it was always summer and the flowers of every season were in bloom.

"Goodness me, how much time I have wasted," sighed Gerda. "It is almost winter. I do not dare rest any longer." And she got up and walked on. Her little feet hurt and she was tired. Water from the cold, autumn mist dripped from the willow trees, as their yellow leaves fell, one by one. Only the blackthorn bush bore fruits now, and they were bitter. Oh, how sombre and grey seemed the wide world.

THE FOURTH STORY, IN WHICH APPEAR A PRINCE AND A PRINCESS

Gerda had to rest. The ground was now covered with snow. A big crow landed near her. He sat a long time wriggling his head and looking at her, "Caw . . . Caw!" he remarked, which in crow language means "Good day." He was kind, and asked the girl why she was out all alone in the lonely winter world.

The word "alone" Gerda understood only too well; and she told the crow her story and asked him if he had seen little Kai.

The crow nodded most thoughtfully and said, "Maybe, maybe!"

"Oh, he is alive!" screamed little Gerda, and almost squeezed the poor bird to death, while she kissed him.

"Be sensible, be sensible," protested the crow. "It may be little Kai I have seen; but if it is, then I am afraid he has forgotten you for the sake of the princess."

"Does he live with a princess?" asked little Gerda.

"Yes, he does," answered the crow, "but are you sure you don't understand crow language? I much prefer speaking it."

"No, I have never learned it; but Grandmother knows it, I wish now that she had taught it to me."

"Never mind, it can't be helped," said the crow. "I shall do my best, which is a lot more than most people do," and the crow told Gerda all that he knew:

"Now in this kingdom, where we are at present, there lives a princess who is immensely clever; she has read all the newspapers in the whole world and forgotten what was written in them, and that is the part that proves how intelligent she is. A few weeks ago, while she was sitting on the throne—and that, people say, is not such an amusing place to sit—she happened to hum a song which has as its chorus the line 'Why shouldn't I get married?'

" 'Why not, indeed?' thought the princess. 'But if I am to get married it must be to a man who can speak up for himself.' She didn't want anyone who just stood about looking distinguished, for such a fellow is boring. She called all her ladies in waiting and told them of her intention. They clapped their hands, and one of them said, 'Oh, how delightful. I had such an idea myself just the other day.' . . . Believe me, everything I tell you is true," declared the crow. "My fiancée is tame, she has the run of the castle and it is from her I got the story." His fiancée was, naturally, another crow, for birds of a feather flock together.

"The newspapers were printed with a border of hearts and the princess' name on the front page. Inside there was a royal proclamation: any good-looking man, regardless of birth, could come to the castle and speak with the princess, and the one who seemed most at home there and spoke the best, she would marry.

"Believe me," said the crow, and shook his head, "as sure as I am sitting here, that proclamation got people out of their houses. They came thick and fast, you have never seen such a crowd. But neither the first nor the second day did the princess find anyone who pleased her. They could all speak well enough as long as they were standing in the street; but as soon as they had entered the castle gates and saw the royal guards, in their silver uniforms, the young men lost their tongues. They didn't get them back, either, when they had to climb the marble stairs, lined with lackeys dressed in gold; or when they finally arrived in the grand hall with the great chandeliers and had to stand in front of the throne on which the princess sat. All they could do was repeat whatever she said; and that she didn't want to hear once more. One should think every one of them had

had his tummy filled with snuff or had fallen into a trance. But as soon as they were down in the streets again they got their tongues back, and all they could do was talk.

"There was a queue, so long that it stretched from beyond the city gate all the way up to the castle. I flew into town to have a look at it. Most of the men got both hungry and thirsty while they waited; the princess didn't even offer them a glass of lukewarm water. Some of the more clever ones had brought sandwiches, but they didn't offer any to their neighbours, for they thought: 'Let him look hungry and the princess won't take him'."

"But Kai! What about Kai?" asked Gerda. "Did he stand in the queue too?"

"Don't be impatient. We are coming to him. Now the third day a little fellow arrived, he didn't have a carriage nor did he come on horseback. No, he came walking straight up to the castle. He was poorly dressed but had bright shining eyes like yours, and the most beautiful long hair."

"That is Kai!" shouted little Gerda, and clapped her hands in joy.

"He had a little knapsack on his back," continued the crow.

"It wasn't a knapsack," interrupted Gerda. "It was his sled.

"Sled or knapsack, it doesn't matter much," said the crow. "I didn't look too closely at him. But this I know from my fiancée: when he entered the castle and saw the royal guards and all the lackeys, they didn't make him the least bit fainthearted. He nodded kindly to them and said, 'It must be boring to spend your life waiting on the stairs, I think I will go inside.' The big hall with its lighted candelabra, its servants carrying golden bowls, while courtiers stood around dressed in their very best, was impressive enough to take away the courage of even the bravest—and, on top of all that, the young man's boots squeaked something wicked—but he did not seem to notice either the elegant hall or his noisy boots."

"It must be Kai," said Gerda. "His boots were new and I know they squeaked, I have heard them myself."

"Well squeak they did," said the crow. "But he walked right up to the princess, who was sitting on a pearl as big as a spinning wheel. Behind her stood all her ladies in waiting with their maids and their maids' maids; and all the gentlemen of the court with their servants and their servants' servants, each of whom, in turn, kept a boy. And the servant's servant's boy, who stood next to the door, always wore slippers and was so proud that one hardly dared look at him!"

"It must have been horrible!" Little Gerda shook her head. "But Kai got the princess anyway?".

"If I hadn't been a crow, I would have taken her and that even though I am engaged. My fiancée tells me that he talks as well as I do when I talk crow language. He said that he hadn't come to propose marriage but only to find out whether she was as clever as everybody said she was. He was satisfied that what he heard was true; and the princess was satisfied with him."

"I am sure it was Kai, for he is so clever, he can work out fractions. Won't you take me to the castle?"

"That is easier said than done," said the crow, and looked thoughtfully at Gerda. "I will talk to my fiancée about it, she might know how we can do it. For I can tell you, it is not easy for a poor little girl like you to get into the castle."

"But I will get in!" protested Gerda. "As soon as Kai hears that I am here he will come and fetch me himself."

"Wait here by the big stone," commanded the crow, wriggled his head, and flew away.

The crow didn't return until dusk. "Caw! Caw!" he said, and alighted on the stone. "I bring you greetings from my fiancée, she sends you this little piece of bread. She took it in the kitchen where there is bread enough, and you must be hungry. It is quite impossible for you to enter the castle. You have bare feet; the guards in their silver uniforms and the lackeys in their golden ones won't allow it. But don't weep, we will get you in anyway. My fiancée knows where the key is kept to the back stairs, and they lead right up to the royal bedchamber."

They entered the royal garden with its long avenue of trees, and watched the lights in the castle being extinguished, one by one. Little Gerda's heart beat both with fear and with longing; she felt as though she were about to do something wrong; and yet all she wanted to do was to find out whether it was little Kai who had won the princess. She was sure it must be he.

In her mind she saw him: his long hair, his lively, clever eyes. She remembered him smiling, as he had when they sat under the rose trees at home. He would be happy to see her. She would tell him of the long journey she had made for his sake; and she would tell him how sad everyone at home was because he had gone; and how they all missed him. At last the crow led her to a little door at the rear of the castle. Oh, she felt so happy and so fearful!

In the middle of the floor stood a tame crow. It was twisting its head and looking at her quizzically. Gerda curtsied as Grandmother had taught her to do.

"My fiancé told me so many nice things about you. He has narrated your *vita* as it is called. I have found the story very touching!" They had reached the stairs. "There is a lamp," she said, and nodded towards a chest, on which one was burning. "You carry it. I shall walk ahead and show the way."

"I think someone is coming," whispered Gerda. There was a whirling, rushing sound; and on the wall were strange shadows of horses with flying manes, dogs and falcons, servants and hunters.

"Oh they are only dreams," said the crow. "They have come to fetch their royal masters. That is only lucky for us; the easier it will be for you to have a good look at them while they are sleeping. But remember, when you gain honour and position, to be grateful and not forget those who helped you get it."

"That is no way to talk," grumbled the wild crow.

Now they entered the first of the great halls. The walls were covered with pink satin and decorated with artificial flowers. The shadows of the dreams reappeared, but they flew past so quickly that Gerda did not even get a chance to see whether Kai was mounted on one of the horses. Each hall they passed through was more magnificent than the one before it. At last they came to the royal bedchamber. The ceiling looked like the top of a large palm tree with glass leaves; from the centre of it hung eight ropes of pure gold, attached to them were the two little beds that the royal couple slept in. Each bed was shaped like a lily; in the white lily slept the princess, and in the red lily the young man who had won her. Gerda peeped into it and saw a head of long brown hair.

"It is Kai!" she shrieked with joy.

The dreams returned as fast as the wind and the young boy woke. Gerda held the lamp up a little higher. It wasn't Kai!

The prince was young and handsome, but only his hair was like little Kai's. The princess sat up in the little white lily bed and asked what was the matter.

Gerda started to cry; and between her sobs, she told her story and explained how the crows had helped her.

"You poor thing!" said the prince. The princess said the same and she did not scold the crows. "They should have a reward!" exclaimed the prince, although he added that he hoped they wouldn't do such a thing again.

"Which would you prefer," began the princess, "to be free or to be given permanent positions as Royal Court Crows with first choice of all left-overs?"

Both the crows curtsied and said they preferred permanent positions at court. After all, they had to think of their old age. "To be secure is better than to fly," they said.

The prince got out of his bed and let Gerda sleep in it; he could hardly do more. She folded her hands and thought, "How good all animals and human beings are!" Then she closed her eyes and slept. The dreams returned and this time they looked like angels. They were drawing a sled and on it sat little Kai. But that was only a dream and it was gone as soon as she awoke.

In the morning Gerda was dressed from head to toe in silk and velvet; and the little prince and princess begged her to stay with them. But she asked only for a little carriage and a horse and some boots, so that she could continue on her journey out in the wide world to find Kai.

She was given not only new boots but a muff as well, and good warm clothes. When she was ready to leave, a fine carriage of the purest gold drove up in front of the castle. The coat of arms of the princess was on the door, and not only was there a coachman to drive her, but a servant stood on the back of the carriage and two little soldiers rode in front. The prince and the princess themselves helped her into the carriage and wished her luck.

Her friend, the wild crow, although he had just got married, decided that he would travel with her the first few miles. They sat beside each other, for the crow said he would be sick if he had to ride sitting backwards. His wife stood at the gate and flapped her wings; she had had a headache since she had become a Royal Court Crow, besides, she had over-eaten. The carriage was lined with candy, and on the seat across from Gerda was a basket of fruit.

"Good-bye, good-bye!" shouted the little prince and princess; and Gerda wept, for she had grown fond of them, and the crow wept too. When they had driven a little way the crow said good-bye, and that was even harder to bear. He flew up into a tall tree and sat there waving with his black wings until he could no longer see the carriage that glistened as though it were made of sunlight.

THE FIFTH STORY, WHICH IS ABOUT THE ROBBER GIRL

They were driving through a great dark forest, and the golden carriage shone like a flame right in the robbers' eyes, and they couldn't bear it.

"Gold! Gold!" they screamed as they came rushing out of the woods. They grabbed hold of the horses and killed the coachman, the servant, and the soldiers; then they dragged little Gerda out of the carriage.

"She is lovely and fat, I bet she has been fed on nuts," said an old robber woman; she had a beard and eyebrows so big and bushy that they almost hid her eyes. "She will taste as good as a lamb," and the robber woman took a long shining knife from her belt; it was horrible to look at.

"Ouch!" screamed the old hag, for just at that moment she had been bitten in the ear by her own little daughter, whom she carried on her back. The child was such a wild and naughty creature that it was a marvel. "Ouch!" the woman cried again, and missed her chance to kill Gerda.

"The girl is to play with me!" declared the little robber girl. "But she is to give me her muff and her dress and sleep in my bed with me." And just to make certain that her mother had understood her, she bit her again as hard as she could.

The robber woman turned and leapt into the air from the pain; and all the robbers laughed, while one of them said, "Look how she dances with her brat!"

"I want to drive in the carriage!" cried the little robber girl, and she could not be stopped, for she was both stubborn and spoiled. Side by side, she and Gerda sat, and the carriage was driven deeper and deeper into the forest.

The little robber girl was as tall as Gerda but much stronger. Her skin had been tanned by the sun. Her eyes were black and looked sad. Putting her arms around Gerda, she said, "I won't let them kill you, as long as you don't make me angry. Are you a princess?"

"No, I am not," Gerda answered and told her whole story and how much she loved little Kai.

The robber girl looked at her very seriously. She nodded and said, "I won't let them kill you. If ever I do get angry with you, I'll do it myself." Then she dried Gerda's eyes and put her own hands inside the soft, warm muff.

At last the carriage stopped; they had come to the robber's castle. The walls were cracked and the windows broken. Crows and ravens flew in and out of the holes in the tower. Ferocious big dogs, who looked as if they could eat human beings, ran about in the courtyard. They sprang in the air, but they didn't bark—that wasn't allowed.

In the middle of the great hall a fire burned. The smoke drifted up among the blackened rafters; how it got out was its own business. A big copper kettle filled with soup hung over the fire, and next to it, on spits, hares and rabbits were being roasted.

"You are going to sleep with me and all my pets," said the little robber girl. And when they had finished eating she dragged Gerda over to a corner of the hall. There on poles sat almost a hundred doves. They appeared to be sleeping, but some turned their heads as the girls approached.

"They are all mine," said the robber girl, and grabbed one of them by the legs. The dove flapped its wings. "Kiss it," she demanded and shoved the frightened bird right up into Gerda's face.

"See, up there are two wood pigeons," the robber girl explained, and she pointed to a recess in the wall, high above them, which a few wooden bars had turned into a cage. "They would fly away in the cold, but they can't."

Tethered near her bed was a reindeer. "Here is my old sweetheart, bah!" she said and gave his antlers a hard pull. "You have to hold on to him, too; or one leap and he would be away. Every evening I tickle his throat, and that frightens him." From a crack in the wall, she pulled out a knife and let its sharp point glide around the reindeer's neck. In terror, the animal backed away as far as it could and almost fell. That made the robber girl laugh; and she pulled Gerda down into her bed.

"Do you sleep with a knife?" asked Gerda, frightened.

"Always!" replied the robber girl. "You never know what might happen . . . But tell me again the story of little Kai and why you have gone out into the wide world."

Gerda told her story once more; and the wood pigeons cooed. All the doves were asleep. The robber girl threw one of her arms around Gerda—in the other hand, she kept her knife. Soon she was asleep and snoring.

Poor Gerda didn't dare close her eyes. She didn't know whether she was going to live or die. The robbers were sitting around the fire, drinking and singing. The robber girl's mother was so drunk that she turned a somersault. Oh, it was a pretty sight for a young girl to see!

Suddenly one of the wood pigeons cooed. "We have seen little Kai. A white hen was carrying his sled. He was sitting next to the Snow Queen, when she flew low over our forest. We had just come out of our eggs and she breathed on us; all the other young ones died. We, alone, survived. Coo! Coo!"

"What is it you are saying?" cried Gerda. "Where was the Snow Queen going? Do you know?"

"I suppose she went to Lapland, where there always are snow and ice, but ask the reindeer that stands tied by your bed."

"Oh yes, ice and snow are always there; it is a blessed place," sighed the reindeer. "There one can jump and run about freely in the great glittering valleys. The Snow Queen keeps a summer tent there, but her castle is far to the north, near the pole, on an island called Spitsbergen."

"Oh, Kai, little Kai!" mumbled Gerda.

"Lie still," commanded the robber girl, "or I will slit open your stomach!"

In the morning Gerda told her what she had heard from the wood pigeons. The little robber girl looked quite solemn, nodding, she said, "I am sure it is he, I am sure." Then she turned to the reindeer and asked him if he knew where Lapland was.

"Who should know that better than I?" answered the poor animal. "There I was born, there I have run across the great snow fields." And his eyes gleamed, recollecting what he had lost.

"Listen," whispered the little robber girl to Gerda. "All the men are gone. Only Mama is here and she won't leave; but in a little while she will take a drink from the big bottle and then she will take a nap. And then ... I will help you!"

She jumped out of bed, ran over and threw her arms around her mother, pulled her beard, and said, "Oh, my own sweet billy goat, good morning!"

The mother tweaked her daughter's nose, so that it turned both red and blue, but it was all done out of love.

When the mother had drunk from the big bottle, she lay down for her midmorning nap; then the robber girl spoke to the reindeer: "I would have loved to tickle your throat for many a day yet, for you look so funny when I do it. But never mind, I will let you loose so that you can run back to Lapland; but you are to take the little girl with you and bring her to the Snow Queen's palace where her playmate is. I know you have heard

everything she said, for you are always eavesdropping."

The reindeer leaped into the air out of pure joy. The robber girl lifted Gerda up on the animal's back and tied her there so she wouldn't fall off; and she even gave her a little pillow to sit on. "I don't really care about your boots, you need them," she said. "It is cold where you are going. But the muff I am keeping, for it is so soft and nice. But you shan't freeze, I will give you my mother's great big mittens; they will keep you warm all the way up to your elbows. Here, put them on! Now your hands look as ugly as my mother's."

Gerda cried from happiness.

"I don't like all your tears," scolded the little robber girl. "You should look happy now. Here are two loaves of bread and a ham, so you won't go hungry," she said as she tied the bread and the ham on the back of the reindeer; then she opened the door and called all the big dogs in. She cut the rope that tethered the reindeer and said in parting, "Run along, but take good care of the little girl!"

Gerda waved good-bye with her great big mittens, and away they went, through the forest and across the great plains, as fast as they could. They heard the wolves howl and the ravens cry; and suddenly the sky was all filled with light.

"There are the old northern lights," said the reindeer. "Look how they shine!"

Still they went on both day and night: farther and farther north.

The bread was eaten and the ham was eaten; and then they were in Lapland.

THE SIXTH STORY: THE LAPP WOMAN AND THE FINNISH WOMAN

They stopped before a little cottage; it was a wretched little hovel: the roof went all the way down to the ground and the doorway was so low that you had to creep through it on all fours. The only person at home was an old Lapp woman who was busy frying some fish over an oil lamp. The reindeer told her Gerda's story; but first he had told his own, because he thought that was more interesting. Poor Gerda was so cold that she couldn't even talk.

"Oh, you poor things!" said the Lapp woman. "You have far to go yet. It is more than a hundred miles from here to the camp of the Snow Queen.

She amuses herself by shooting fireworks off every night. I shall give you an introduction to the Finnish woman who lives up there. She knows more about it all than I do and will be able to help you. Paper I have none of, so I will write on a dried codfish."

When little Gerda had eaten and was warm again, the Lapp woman wrote a few words on a dried codfish and told Gerda not to lose it. Then she tied her on the reindeer's back again and away they ran.

Whish . . . Whish . . . it said up in the sky as the northern lights flickered and flared; they were the Snow Queen's fireworks. At last they came to the Finnish woman's house; they had to knock on the chimney, for the door was so small that they couldn't find it.

Goodness me, it was hot inside! The Finnish woman walked around almost naked. She pulled off both Gerda's boots and her mittens so that the heat would not be unbearable for her. The reindeer got a piece of ice to put on its head. Then the Finnish woman read what was written on the codfish; she read it three times and then she knew it by heart. The fish she put in the pot that was boiling over the fire. It could be eaten, and she never wasted anything. The reindeer told first of his own adventures and then of Gerda's. The Finnish woman squinted her intelligent eyes but didn't utter a word.

"You are so clever," said the reindeer finally. "I know you can tie all the winds of the world into four knots on a single thread. If a sailor loosens the first knot he get a fair wind; if he loosens the second a strong breeze; but if he loosens the third and the fourth knots, then there's such a storm that the trees in the forest are torn up by the roots. Won't you give this little girl a magic drink so that she gains the strength of twelve men and can conquer the Snow Queen?"

"The strength of twelve men," laughed the Finnish woman. "Yes, I should think that would be enough." Then she walked over to a shelf and took down a roll of skin which she spread out on the table. Strange words were written there, and the Finnish woman read and studied till the perspiration ran down her forehead.

The reindeer begged her again to help little Gerda; and Gerda looked up at her with eyes filled with tears. The Finish woman winked, then drew the reindeer into a corner, where she whispered to him while she gave him another piece of ice for his head.

"Little Kai is in the Snow Queen's palace and is quite satisfied with being there; he thinks it is the best place in the whole world. This is because he has got a sliver of glass in his heart and two grains of the same in his eyes. As long as they are there he will never be human again, and the Snow Queen will keep her power over him."

"But can't you give Gerda some kind of power so that she can take out the glass?" asked the reindeer.

"I can't give her any more power than she already has! Don't you understand how great it is? Don't you see how men and animals must serve her; how else could she have come so far, walking on her bare feet? But she must never learn of her power; it is in her heart, for she is a sweet and innocent child. If she herself cannot get into the Snow Queen's palace and free Kai from the glass splinters in his eyes and his heart, how can we help her? Two miles from here begin the gardens of the Snow Queen. Carry Gerda there and set her down by the bush with the red berries, then come right back here and don't stand about gossiping." The Finnish woman lifted Gerda back on the reindeer's back, and he ran as fast as he could.

"I don't have my boots on, and I forgot the mittens," cried Gerda when she felt the cold making her naked feet smart. But the reindeer did not dare return. He ran on until he came to the bush with the red berries. There he put Gerda down and kissed her on her mouth; two tears ran down the animal's cheeks; then he leaped and ran back to the Finnish woman as fast as he could.

There stood poor Gerda, barefooted and without mittens on, in the intense arctic cold. She entered the Snow Queen's garden and ran as fast as she could in the direction of the palace. A whole regiment of snowflakes were advancing towards her. They had not come from the sky, for that was cloudless and illuminated by northern lights. The snowflakes flew just above the snow-covered earth; and as they came nearer they grew in size. Gerda remembered how they had looked when seen through a magnifying glass, but these were really big and not at all pretty. They were the Snow Queen's guard. And what strange creatures they were! Some of them looked like ugly little porcupines, others like bunches of snakes all twisted together, and some like little bears with bristly fur. All of the snowflakes were brilliantly white and terribly alive.

Little Gerda stopped and said the Lord's Prayer. It was so cold that she could see her own breath; it came like a fine white smoke from her mouth, then it became more and more solid and formed itself into little angels that grew as soon as they touched the ground; all of them had helmets on their

heads and shields and spears in their hands. When Gerda had finished saying her prayer a whole legion of little angels stood around her. They threw their spears at the snow monsters, and they splintered into hundreds of pieces. Little Gerda walked on unafraid, and the angels caressed her little feet and hands so she did not feel the cold.

But now we must hear what happened to little Kai. He was not thinking of Gerda—and even if he had been, he could not have imagined that she could be standing right outside the palace.

THE SEVENTH STORY: WHAT HAPPENED IN THE SNOW QUEEN'S PALACE AND AFTERWARDS

The walls of the palace were snowdrifts, and in them the sharp winds had made windows and doors. There were a hundred halls and several of them were many miles long. All were lighted by the bright glare of the northern lights; they were huge, empty, and terrifyingly cold. Here no one had ever gathered for a bit of innocent fun; not even a dance for polar bears, where they might have walked on their hind legs in the manner of man and the wind could have produced the music. No one had ever been invited in for a little game of cards, with something good to eat and a bit of not too malicious gossip; nor had there ever been a tea party for young white lady foxes. No, empty, vast, and cold was the Snow Queen's palace.

The northern lights burned so precisely that you could tell to the very second when they would be at their highest and their lowest points. In the centre of that enormous snow hall was a frozen lake. It had cracked into thousands of pieces and every one of them was shaped exactly like all the others. In the middle of the lake was the throne of the Snow Queen. Here she sat when she was at home. She called the lake the Mirror of Reason, and declared that it was the finest mirror in the world.

Little Kai was blue—indeed, almost black—from the cold; but he did not feel it, for the Snow Queen had kissed all feeling of coldness out of him, and his heart had almost turned into a lump of ice. He sat arranging and rearranging pieces of ice into patterns. He called this the Game of Reason; and because of the splinters in his eyes, he thought that what he was doing was of great importance, although it was no different from playing with wooden bricks, which he had done when he could hardly talk.

He wanted to put the pieces of ice together in such a way that they formed a certain word, but he could not remember exactly what that word was. The word that he could not remember was "eternity". The Snow Queen had told him that if he could place the pieces of ice so that they spelled that word, then he would be his own master and she would give him the whole world and a new pair of skates; but, however much he tried, he couldn't do it.

"I am going to the warm countries," the Snow Queen had announced that morning. "I want to look into the boiling black pots." By "black pots", she meant the volcanoes, Vesuvius and Etna. "I will chalk their peaks a bit. It will do them good to be refreshed; ice is pleasant as a dessert after oranges and lemons."

The Snow Queen flew away and Kai was left alone in the endless hall. He sat pondering his patterns of ice, thinking and thinking; he sat so still one might have believed that he was frozen to death.

Little Gerda entered the castle. The winds whipped her face; but she said her bedtime prayers, and they lay down to sleep. She came into the vast, empty cold hall; and there was Kai!

She ran up to him and threw her arms around him, while she exclaimed jubilantly: "Kai, sweet little Kai! At last, I have found you!"

But Kai sat still and stiff and cold; then little Gerda cried and her tears fell on Kai's breast. The warmth penetrated to his heart and melted both the ice and the glass splinter in it. He looked at her, and she sang the psalm they had once sung together:

> Seek with the humble and the meek,
> In the dust for Our Saviour weep,
> In the valleys the roses grow
> There Child Jesus you shall know

Kai burst into tears and wept so much that the grains of glass in his eyes were washed away.

"Gerda, sweet Gerda!" he shouted joyfully. Now he remembered her. "Where have you been so long? And where have I been?" Kai looked around him. "How cold it is here! How empty, and how huge!" And he held on to Gerda who was so happy that she was both laughing and crying. And the moment was so joyous that even the pieces of ice could feel it. They started to dance and when they grew tired, they lay down and formed the exact word for which the Snow Queen had promised Kai the whole world and a new pair of skates: Eternity!

Gerda kissed him on his cheeks and the colour came back to them. She kissed his eyes and they became like hers. She kissed his hands and feet, and the blue colour left them and the blood pulsed again through his veins. He was well and strong. Now the Snow Queen could return, it did not matter, for his right to his freedom was written in brilliant pieces of ice.

They took each other by the hand and walked out of the great palace. They talked of Grandmother, and the roses that bloomed on the roof at home. The winds were still; and as they walked, the sun broke through the clouds. When they reached the bush with the red berries the reindeer was waiting there for them. He had brought another young reindeer with him and her udder was bursting with milk. The two children drank from it and the reindeer kissed them. Then they rode on the backs of the reindeer to the home of the Finnish woman, where they got warm; and while they ate were given instruction for the homeward journey. They arrived at the Lapp woman's. She had sewn warm clothes for them and had already harnessed her sled.

The two reindeer accompanied them to the border of Lapland. There the green grass started to break through the snow and they could not use the sled any longer. They said good-bye to the reindeer and to the Lapp woman. Soon they heard the twitter of the first birds of spring and in the woods the trees were budding.

They met a young girl wearing a red hat and riding a magnificent horse. Gerda recognized the animal, for it was one of the horses that had drawn her golden carriage. The girl had two pistols stuck in her belt; it was the little robber girl, who had got tired of staying at home and now was on her way out into the wide world. She recognized Gerda immediately and the two of them were so happy to see each other.

"You are a fine one," she said to Kai, "running about as you did. I wonder if you are worth going to the end of the world for?" Gerda touched her cheek and asked her if she knew what had happened to the prince and the princess. "They have gone travelling in foreign lands," answered the robber girl.

"And what about the crow?"

"The wild crow is dead," said the girl. "His tame wife has become a widow, she wears a black wool thread around her leg. She thinks mourning becomes her, but it is all nonsense. Now tell me what happened to you and how you managed to find him!"

And both Gerda and Kai told her everything.

"Well, the end was as good as the beginning," said the robber girl, and took each of them by the hand and promised that if she ever came through the town where they lived she would come and visit them. Then she rode away out into the wide world.

Kai and Gerda walked on, hand in hand. Now it was really spring: everywhere it was green. Churchbells were ringing. They recognized the towers. They were approaching a city and it was their own. Soon they were climbing the worn stairs to Grandmother's room. Nothing in it had changed. The clock said: "Tick-tack . . ." and the hands moved. As they stepped through the doorway they realized that they had grown: they were no longer children.

The roses were blooming in the wooden boxes and the window was open. There were the little stools they used to sit on. Still holding each other's hands, they sat down, and all memory of the Snow Queen's palace and its hollow splendour disappeared: Grandmother sat in the sunshine, reading aloud from her Bible: *"Whosoever shall not receive the Kingdom of Heaven as a little child shall not enter therein."*

Kai and Gerda looked into each other's eyes and suddenly they understood the words of the psalm:

In the valleys roses grow
There Child Jesus you shall know.

They were grownups, and yet in their hearts children. And it was summer: a warm, glorious summer!

The Darning Needle

Once upon a time there was a darning needle who was so refined that she was convinced she was a sewing needle.

"Be careful! Watch what you are holding!" she shouted to the fingers who had picked her up. "I am so fine and thin that if I fall on the floor you will never be able to find me again."

"Don't overdo it," snarled the fingers, and squeezed her around the waist.

"Look, I am travelling with a retinue," said the needle. She was referring to the thread that trailed behind her but wasn't knotted. The fingers steered the needle toward the cook's slippers; the leather had split and had to be sewn.

"This is vulgar work," complained the darning needle. "I can't get through it. I shall break! I shall break!" And then she broke. "Didn't I tell you I was too fine?" she whined.

Had it been up to the fingers, then the darning needle would have been thrown away; but they had to mind the cook, so they dipped the needle in hot sealing wax and stuck it into the cook's blouse.

"Now I have become a brooch," exclaimed the darning needle. "I have always felt that I was born to be something better. When you are something, you always become something." Then she laughed inside herself; for you cannot see from the outside when a needle is laughing.

There she sat as proudly as if she were looking out at the world from a seat in a golden carriage.

"May I take the liberty of asking you whether you are made of gold?" The darning needle was talking to her neighbour, a pin. "You look very handsome, and you have a head, even though it is small. Take my advice and let it grow a little bigger; not everyone can be so fortunate as to be dipped in sealing wax." The darning needle drew herself up a little too proudly; for she fell out of the blouse and down into the sink, at exactly the moment when the cook was rinsing it out.

"Here we go, travelling!" exlaimed the darning needle. "I hope I won't get lost." But she did get lost.

"I am too fine for this world," she remarked when she finally came to rest at the bottom of a gutter. "But I know who I am and where I come from, and that is always something." And the darning needle kept her back straight and remained cheerful.

All sorts of garbage were floating by above her: twigs, straw, pieces of newspaper. "Look how they sail on," mumbled the needle. "They have no idea what is sticking up right beneath them; and I can stick! Look at that old twig; it does not think about anything else in the whole world but twigs, because it is one. There goes a straw. . . . Look how it turns first one way and then the other. . . . Don't think so much of yourself, or you may get hurt on the curbstone. . . . There comes a newspaper; everything written in it is already forgotten, and yet it spreads itself out as if it were of great importance. . . . I sit patiently and wait. I know who I am and that I shall never change."

One day something shiny came to rest near the needle. It was a glass splinter from a broken bottle, but the darning needle thought it was a diamond. Since it glittered so nicely, she decided to converse with it. She introduced herself as a brooch. "I presume you are a diamond," she said. And the glass splinter hastily agreed that he was "something of that nature". Each of them believed that the other was valuable, and so they began to discuss how proud and haughty the rest of the world was.

"I have lived in a box belonging to a young lady," began the darning needle. "She was a cook, and she had five fingers on each hand. There never existed creatures so conceited as those fingers; and yet they were only there to take me out of the box and put me back."

"Did they shine?" asked the glass splinter.

"Shine!" sneered the needle. "Oh, they were haughty. They were five brothers: all born fingers; and they stood in a row next to each other, in spite of there being so much difference in their sizes. The one who resembled the others the least was the thumb. He was short and fat and had only one joint in his back, so he could only bend once. He always kept to himself, and said that if he were ever chopped off a man's hand that man could not become a soldier. The other four fingers stuck together. The first one was always pointing at everything, and if the cook wanted to find out whether a sauce was too sour or too sweet, that finger was stuck into the dish or the pot; and it guided the pen when she wrote. The next finger was the tallest and he looked down on the others. The third one wore a gold ring around his stomach; and the fourth one never did anything, and that's what he was proud of. They bragged and boasted day and night! That was all they could do well. And I dived into the sink."

"And here we sit and glitter," said the glass splinter. At that moment the water in the gutter suddenly rose and went over its sides, taking the glass splinter with it.

"Well, he got his advancement," said the darning needle. "I was left behind, but I am too refined to complain. That, too, is a form of pride but it is respectable." And the needle kept her back straight and went on thinking.

"I am almost convinced that a sun ray must have given birth to me. When I think of it, the sun is always searching for me underneath the water; but I am so fine that my own mother cannot find me. If I had my old eye—the one that was broken off—I think I would cry. No, I wouldn't anyway, crying is so vulgar."

One day some street urchins were rummaging in the gutter. They found nails, coins, and the like. They made themselves filthy and they enjoyed doing it.

"Ow!" cried one of the boys. The needle had pricked him. "What kind of a fellow are you?"

"Fellow! I am a lady!" protested the darning needle. The sealing wax had long since worn off and she was black; but black things look thinner, so she thought that now she was even finer than before.

"Here comes an eggshell!" shouted another boy, and stuck the pin into it.

"How well it becomes a black needle to stand before a white sail! Everyone can see me. I hope I shan't get seasick and throw up, that is so undignified. There is no remedy against seasickness better than an iron stomach, and the awareness of being just a bit above the common herd. I feel much better. The more refined one is, the more one can bear."

"Crash!" said the eggshell. A wagon wheel had rolled over it.

"Ow!" cried the darning needle. "Something is pressing against me. I think I am going to be seasick after all. I fear I will break!"

But it didn't break, even though a loaded wagon drove over it. There it lay, lengthwise in the gutter; and there we'll leave it.

The Steadfast Tin Soldier

Once there were five and twenty tin soldiers. They were all brothers because they had been made from the same old tin spoon. With their rifles sticking up over their shoulders, they stood at attention, looking straight ahead, in their handsome red and blue uniforms.

"Tin soldiers!" were the first words they heard in this world; and they had been shouted happily by a little boy who was clapping his hands because he had received them as a birthday gift. He took them immediately out of the box they had come in and set them on the table. They were all exactly alike except one, who was different from the others because he was missing a leg. He had been the last one to be cast and there had not been enough tin. But he stood as firm and steadfast on his one leg as the others did on their two. He is the hero of our story.

Of all the many toys on the table, the one you noticed first was a pasteboard castle. It was a little replica of a real castle, and through its windows you could see right into its handsomely painted halls. In front of the castle was a little lake surrounded by trees; in it swans swam and looked at their own reflections because the lake was a glass mirror. It was all very lovely; but the most charming part of the castle was its mistress. She was a little paper doll and she was standing in the entrance dressed like a ballerina. She had a skirt of white muslin and a blue ribbon draped over her shoulder, which was fastened with a spangle that was almost as large as

98

her face. The little lady had her arms stretched out, as if she were going to embrace someone. She stood on one leg, and at that on her toes, for she was a ballet dancer; the other, she held up behind her, in such a way that it disappeared under her skirt; and therefore the soldier thought that she was one-legged like himself.

"She would be a perfect wife for me," he thought. "But I am afraid she is above me. She has a castle and I have only a box that I must share with twenty-four soldiers; that wouldn't do for her. Still, I would like to make her acquaintance." And the soldier lay down full length behind a snuffbox; from there he could look at the young lady, who was able to stand on the toes of only one leg without losing her balance.

Later in the evening, when it was the children's bedtime, all the other tin soldiers were put back in the box. When the house was quiet and everyone had gone to bed, the toys began to play. They played house, and hide-and-seek, and held a ball. The four and twenty tin soldiers rattled inside their box; they wanted to play too, but they couldn't get the lid off. The nutcracker turned somersaults, and the slate pencil wrote on the blackboard. They made so much noise that the canary woke up and recited his opinion of them all in verse. The only ones who didn't move were the ballerina and the soldier. She stood as steadfast on the toes of her one leg as the soldier did on his. His eyes never left her, not even for a moment did he blink or turn away.

The clock struck twelve. Pop! The lid of the snuffbox opened and out jumped a troll. It was a jack-in-the-box.

"Tin soldier," screamed the little black troll, "keep your eyes to yourself."

The tin soldier acted as if he hadn't heard the remark.

"You wait till tomorrow!" threatened the troll, and disappeared back into its box.

The next morning when the children were up and dressed, the little boy put the one-legged soldier on the window sill. It's hard to tell whether it was the troll or just the wind that caused the window to open suddenly and the soldier to fall out of it. He dropped down three stories to the street and his bayonet stuck in the earth between two cobblestones.

The boy and the maid came down to look for him and, though they almost stepped on him, they didn't see him. If only the tin soldier had shouted, "Here I am!" they would have found him; but he thought it improper to shout when in uniform.

It began to rain; first one drop fell and then another and soon it was pouring. When the shower was over two urchins came by. "Look," said one of them, "there is a tin soldier. He will do as a sailor."

The boys made a boat out of a newspaper, put the tin soldier on board, and let it sail in the gutter. Away it went, for it had rained so hard that the gutter was a raging torrent. The boys ran along on the pavement, clapping their hands. The boat dipped and turned in the waves. The tin soldier trembled and quaked inside himself; but outside, he stood as steadfast as ever, shouldering his gun and looking straight ahead.

Now the gutter was covered by a board. It was as dark as it had been inside the box, but there he had had four and twenty comrades. "I wonder how it will all end," thought the soldier. "I am sure it's all the troll's doing. If only the ballerina were here, then I wouldn't care if it were twice as dark as pitch."

A big water rat that lived in the gutter came up behind the boat and shouted, "Have you got a passport? Give me your passport!"

The tin soldier didn't answer but held more firmly on to his rifle. The current became stronger, and the boat gathered speed. The rat swam after him; it was so angry that it gnashed its teeth. "Stop him! Stop him!" the rat shouted to two pieces of straw and a little twig. "Stop him! He hasn't got a passport and he won't pay duty!"

The current ran swifter and swifter. The tin soldier could see light ahead; he was coming out of the tunnel. But at the same moment he heard a strange roaring sound. It was frightening enough to make the bravest man cringe. At the end of the tunnel the gutter emptied into one of the canals of the harbour. If you can imagine it, it would be the same as for a human being to be thrown down a great waterfall into the sea.

There was no hope of stopping the boat. The poor tin soldier stood as steady as ever, he did not flinch. The boat spun around four times and became filled to the brim with water. It was doomed, the paper began to fall apart; the tin soldier was standing in water up to his neck. He thought of the ballerina, whom he would never see again, and two lines from a poem ran through his mind.

> Fare thee well, my warrior bold,
> Death comes so swift and cold.

The paper fell apart and the tin soldier would have sunk down into the mud at the bottom of the canal had not a greedy fish swallowed him just at that moment.

Here it was even darker than it had been in the sewer; the fish's stomach was terribly narrow, but the soldier lay there as steadfast as he had stood in the boat, without letting go of his rifle.

The fish darted and dashed in the wildest manner; then suddenly it was still. A while later, a ray of light appeared and someone said, "Why, there is a tin soldier." The fish had been caught, taken to the market, and sold. The kitchen maid had found the soldier when she opened the fish up with a big knife, in order to clean it. With her thumb and her index finger she picked the tin soldier up by the waist and carried him into the living room, so that everyone could admire the strange traveller who had journeyed inside the belly of a fish. But the tin soldier was not proud of his adventures.

How strange the world is! He was back in the same room that he had left in the morning; and he had been put down on the table among the toys he knew. There stood the cardboard castle and the little ballerina. She was still standing on one leg, the other she had lifted high into the air. She was as steadfast as he was. It touched the soldier's heart and he almost cried tin tears—and would have, had it not been so undignified. He looked at her and she at him, but never a word passed between them.

Suddenly one of the little boys grabbed the soldier, opened the stove, and threw him in. The child couldn't explain why he had done it; there's no question but that the jack-in-the-box had had something to do with it.

The tin soldier stood illuminated by the flames that leaped around him. He did not know whether the great heat he felt was caused by his love or the fire. The colours of his uniform had disappeared, and who could tell whether it was from sorrow or his trip through the water? He looked at the ballerina, and she looked at him. He could feel that he was melting; but he held on as steadfastly as ever to his gun and kept his gaze on the little ballerina in front of the castle.

The door of the room was opened, a breeze caught the little dancer and like a sylph she flew right into the stove. She flared up and was gone. The soldier melted. The next day when the maid emptied the stove, she found a little tin heart, which was all that was left of him. Among the ashes lay the metal spangle from the ballerina's dress; it had been burned as black as coal.

The Little Match Girl

It was dreadfully cold, snowing, and turning dark. It was the last evening of the year, New Year's Eve. In this cold and darkness walked a little girl. She was poor and both her head and feet were bare. Oh, she had had a pair of slippers when she left home; but they had been too big for her — in truth, they had belonged to her mother. The little one had lost them while hurrying across the street to get out of the way of two carriages that had been driving along awfully fast. One of the slippers she could not find, and the other had been snatched by a boy who, laughingly, shouted that he would use it as a cradle when he had a child of his own.

Now the little girl walked barefoot through the streets. Her feet were swollen and red from the cold. She was carrying a little bundle of matches in her hand and had more in her apron pocket. No one had bought any all day, or given her so much as a penny. Cold and hungry, she walked through the city; cowed by life, the poor thing!

The snowflakes fell on her long yellow hair that curled so prettily at the neck, but to such things she never gave a thought. From every window of every house, light shone, and one could smell the geese roasting all the way out in the street. It was, after all, New Year's Eve; and this she did think about.

In a little recess between two houses she sat down and tucked her feet under her. But now she was even colder. She didn't dare go home because she had sold no matches and was frightened that her father might beat her. Besides, her home was almost as cold as the street. She lived in an attic, right under a tile roof. The wind whistled through it, even though they had tried to close the worst of the holes and cracks with straw and old rags.

Her little hands were numb from cold. If only she dared strike a match, she could warm them a little. She took one and struck it against the brick wall of the house; it lighted! Oh, how warm it was and how clearly it burned like a little candle. She held her hand around it. How strange! It seemed that the match had become a big iron stove with brass fixtures. Oh, how blessedly warm it was! She stretched out her legs so that they, too, could get warm, but at that moment the stove disappeared and she was sitting alone with a burned-out match in her hand.

She struck another match. Its flame illuminated the wall and it became as transparent as a veil: she could see right into the house. She saw the table spread with a damask cloth and set with the finest porcelain. In the centre, on a dish, lay a roasted goose stuffed with apples and prunes! But what was even more wonderful: the goose—although a fork and knife were stuck in its back—had jumped off the table and was waddling towards her. The little girl stretched out her arms and the match burned out. Her hands touched the cold, solid walls of the house.

She lit a third match. The flame flared up and she was sitting under a Christmas tree that was much larger and more beautifully decorated than the one she had seen through the glass doors at the rich merchant's on Christmas Eve. Thousands of candles burned on its green branches, and colourful pictures like the ones you can see in shop windows were looking down at her. She smiled up at them; but then the match burned itself out, and the candles of the Christmas tree became the stars in the sky. A shooting star drew a line of fire across the dark heavens.

"Someone is dying," whispered the little girl. Her grandmother, who was dead, was the only person who had ever loved or been kind to the child; and she had told her that a shooting star was the soul of a human being travelling to God.

She struck yet another match against the wall and in its blaze she saw her grandmother, so sweet, so blessedly kind.

"Grandmother!" shouted the little one. "Take me with you! I know you will disappear when the match goes out, just like the warm stove, the goose, and the beautiful Christmas tree." Quickly, she lighted all the matches she had left in her hand, so that her grandmother could not leave.

And the matches burned with such a clear, strong flame that the night became as light as day. Never had her grandmother looked so beautiful. She lifted the little girl in her arms and flew with her to where there is neither cold nor hunger nor fear: up to God.

In the cold morning the little girl was found. Her cheeks were red and she was smiling. She was dead. She had frozen to death on the last evening of the old year. The sun on New Year's Day shone down on the little corpse; her lap was filled with burned-out matches.

"She had been trying to warm herself," people said. And no one knew the sweet visions she had seen, or in what glory she and her grandmother had passed into a truly new year.

Little Claus and Big Claus

Once upon a time there lived in a village two men who had the same name; they were both called Claus. But one of them owned four horses, while the other had only one; so to tell them apart the richer man was called Big Claus and the poorer one Little Claus. Now let's hear what happened to the two of them because that's a real story!

Six days a week Little Claus had to work for Big Claus and lend him his horse; and in return Big Claus had to let Little Claus borrow his four horses on Sunday. One day a week Little Claus felt as if all the horses belonged to him, and he would crack his whip in the air and shout orders to them merrily.

One morning when the sun was shining brightly and the villagers, all dressed up in their Sunday best, with their prayer books under their arms, were passing his field, Little Claus cracked his whip in the air, whistled, and called out very loudly, "Gee up, all my horses!"

"You may not say that!" exclaimed Big Claus. "Only one of the horses is yours."

But Little Claus forgot very quickly what Big Claus had said, and the next time someone went by and nodded kindly in his direction, he shouted, "Gee up, all my horses!"

Big Claus turned around and shouted: "I beg you for the last time not to call all those horses yours because if you do it once more I'll take the

107

mallet that I use to drive in the stake for tethering my four horses and hit your one horse so hard that it will drop dead on the spot."

"I promise never to say it again," said Little Claus meekly. But the words were hardly out of his mouth when still another group of churchgoers stopped to watch him plough. They smiled and said good morning in a very friendly way. "What a fine figure I must cut, driving five horses," he thought; and without realizing what he was doing, he cracked the whip and cried, "Gee up, all my horses!"

"I'll give your horse gee up!" screamed Big Claus in a rage; and he took his tethering mallet and hit Little Claus's only horse so hard on the forehead that it fell down quite dead.

"Poor me!" cried Little Claus. "Now I haven't got a horse at all!" And he sat down and wept. But as there was nothing else to do he flayed the horse and hung the hide up to dry. When the wind had done its work, Little Claus put the hide in a sack and set off for town to sell it in the market place.

It was a long way and the road led through a forest. The weather turned bad and among the dark shadows Little Claus lost his way. He turned first in one direction and then in another. Finally he did find his way again; but by then it was late afternoon and too late to reach town before nightfall.

Not far from the road he saw a farmhouse. The shutters were closed but above them there shone tiny streams of light. "There I may ask for shelter for the night," Little Claus thought, and made his way to the front door and knocked.

The farmer's wife answered the door, but when she heard what he wanted she shook her head. "You'll have to go away," she ordered. "My husband isn't home and I cannot allow a stranger to come in."

"Then I'll have to sleep outside," said Little Claus. The farmer's wife shut the door without another word; and Little Claus looked about him. Near the house was a haystack, and between that and the dwelling there was a shed with a flat thatched roof.

"I'll stretch out on that," Little Claus mumbled, looking at the roof. "It will make a fine bed and I doubt if the stork will fly down and bite me." The latter was said in jest because there was a stork's nest on the roof of the farmhouse.

Little Claus climbed up on the roof of the shack; and while he was twisting and turning to make himself comfortable, he realized that from where he lay he could see right into the kitchen of the farmhouse because,

at the top, the shutters did not close tightly.

A fine white linen cloth covered the large table and on it were not only a roast and wine but a platter of fish as well. On one side of the table sat the farmer's wife and on the other the deacon; and while she filled his glass with wine, he filled himself with fish because that was his favourite food.

"If only I had been invited too!" Little Claus sighed, and pushed himself as near to the window as he could without touching the shutters. There was a cake on the table too; this was better than a party, it was a feast!

He heard someone galloping on the road; he turned and saw the rider: it was the farmer coming home.

Now this farmer was known for two things: one, that he was a good fellow, and the other, that he suffered from a strange disease; he couldn't bear the sight of a deacon. One glance and he went into a rage. And that, of course, was the reason why the deacon had come visiting on a day when the farmer wasn't at home; and that too was why the farmer's wife had made the most delicious food she could for her guest.

When they heard the farmer riding up to the door of his house, both the farmer's wife and the deacon were terrified; and she told him to climb into a large empty chest that stood in the corner. The poor man, trembling with fear, obeyed her. Then the woman hid all the food and the wine in the oven, for she knew that if her husband saw all the delicacies he was certain to ask her why she had made them.

"Ow!" groaned Little Claus when he saw the last of the food disappear into the bread oven.

"Is there someone up there?" the farmer called, and when he saw Little Claus lying on the roof of the shed he told him to come down. "What were you doing up there?"

Little Claus explained how he had lost his way in the forest and asked the farmer to be allowed to spend the night in his house.

"You are most welcome," said the farmer, who was the kindest of men, as long as there was no deacon in sight. "But first let's have a bite to eat."

The farmer's wife greeted them both very politely, set the table, and served them a large bowl of porridge. The farmer, who was very hungry, ate with relish; but Little Claus kept thinking of all the delicious food in the oven and couldn't swallow a spoonful.

At his feet under the table lay the sack with the horse hide in it. He stepped on the sack and the horse hide squeaked. 'Shhhhhhhh!'

whispered Little Claus to the sack; but at the same time he pressed his foot down on it even harder and it squeaked even louder.

"What have you got in the bag?" asked the farmer.

"Oh, it's only a wizard," Little Claus replied. "He was telling me that there's no reason for us to eat porridge when he has just conjured both fish and meat for us, and even a cake. Look in the oven."

"What!" exclaimed the farmer; and he ran to the oven and opened it. There he saw all the good food that his wife had made for the deacon; and she—not daring to tell him the truth—silently served the roast, the fish, and the cake.

After he had taken a few mouthfuls, Little Claus stepped on the sack again so that the hide squeaked.

"What is the wizard saying now?" asked the farmer eagerly.

"He says that he has conjured three bottles of wine for us and that you will find them in the corner next to the oven."

The farmer's poor wife brought out the wine, which she had hidden, and poured it for Little Claus and her husband, who made so many toasts to each other's health that they were soon very merry. Then the farmer began to think about Little Claus's sack and what a wonderful thing it must be to have a wizard.

"Do you think he could conjure the Devil?" the farmer asked. "For now that I have the courage I wouldn't mind seeing what he looks like."

"Why not?" replied Little Claus. "My wizard will do anything I tell him to . . . Won't you?" he added, stepping on the sack so that it squeaked. Turning to the farmer, Little Claus smiled. "Can't you hear that he said yes? But the Devil has such an ugly face that he's not worth looking at."

"I'm not afraid," said the farmer, and hiccupped. "How terrible can he look?"

"He looks just like a deacon!"

"Pooh!" returned the farmer. "That's worse than I thought! I must confess that I cannot stand the sight of a deacon; but now that I know that it is only the Devil I will be looking at, maybe I can bear it. But don't let him come too near me and let's get it over with before I lose my courage."

"I'll tell my wizard," said Little Claus and stepped on the hide; then he cocked his head as if he were listening to someone.

"What is he saying?" asked the farmer, who could only hear the hide squeak.

"He says that if we go over to the chest in the corner and open it up we shall see the Devil sitting inside. But we must be careful when we lift the lid, not to lift it too high, so the Devil can escape."

"Then you must hold on to the lid while I lift it," whispered the farmer to Little Claus as he tiptoed to the chest in which the deacon was hiding. This poor fellow had heard every word that Little Claus and the farmer had said and was quaking with fear.

The farmer opened the chest no more than an inch or two and peeped inside. "Ah!" he screamed and jumped up, letting the lid fall back into place. "I saw him! He looked exactly like our deacon! It was a dreadful sight!"

After such an experience you need a drink; and Little Claus and the farmer had many, for they drank late into the night.

"You must sell me that wizard," the farmer finally said. "Ask whatever you want for it . . . I'll give you a bushel basket full of money, if that's what you'd like."

"I wouldn't think of it," replied Little Claus. "You have seen for yourself all the marvellous things that wizard can do."

"But I want it with all my heart," begged the farmer; and he kept on pleading with Little Claus until at last he agreed.

"I cannot forget that you gave me a night's lodging," Little Claus said. "Take my wizard, but remember to fill the bushel basket to the very top."

"I shall! I shall!" exclaimed the farmer. "But you must take the chest along too. I won't have it in my house. Who knows but that the Devil isn't still inside it?"

And that's how it happened that Little Claus gave the farmer a sack with a horse hide in it and in return was given not only a bushel full of money and a chest but a wheelbarrow to carry them away.

"Good-bye!" called Little Claus, and off he went.

On the other side of the forest there was a deep river with a current that flowed so swiftly that you could not swim against it. But the river had to be crossed and so a bridge had been built. When Little Claus reached the middle of that bridge, he said very loudly—so the deacon, who was still inside the chest, could hear him —"What's the point of dragging this chest any farther? It's so heavy, you'd think it was filled with stones. I'm all worn out. I know what I'll do, I'll dump the chest into the stream and if the current carries it home to me, all well and good; and if not, it doesn't matter." Then he took hold of the chest and pushed it, as if he were about to lift it out of the wheelbarrow and let it fall into the water.

"No, stop it!" cried the deacon from inside the chest. "Let me out! Please, let me out!"

"Oh!" shouted Little Claus as if he were frightened. "The Devil is still in there. I'd better throw the chest right into the river and drown him."

"No! No!" screamed the deacon. "I'll give you a bushel of money if you'll let me out!"

"That's a different tune," said Little Claus, and opened the chest. The deacon climbed out and shoved the chest into the river. Together Little Claus and the deacon went to the deacon's home, where he gave Little Claus the bushel of coins that he had promised him. Now Little Claus had a whole wheelbarrow full of money.

"That wasn't bad payment for my old horse," he said to himself as he dumped all the coins out on the floor of his own living room. "What a big pile it is! It will annoy Big Claus to find out how rich I have become, all because of my horse. I won't tell him but let him find out for himself."

A few minutes later a boy banged on Big Claus's door and asked him if he could borrow his grain measure for Little Claus.

"I wonder what he is going to use that for," thought Big Claus; and in order to find out he dabbed a bit of tar in the bottom of the measuring pail, which was quite clever of him because when it was returned he found a silver coin stuck to the spot.

"Where did that come from?" shouted Big Claus, and ran as fast as he could to Little Claus's house. When he saw Little Claus in the midst of his riches, he shouted even louder, "Where did you get all that money from?"

"Oh, that was for my horse hide, I sold it last night."

"You were certainly well paid!" said Big Claus; and hurried home where he took an axe and killed all four of his horses; then he flayed them and set off for town with their hides.

"Hides for sale! Hides for sale! Who wants to buy hides?" Big Claus shouted from street to street.

All the shoemakers and tanners came out of their workshops to ask him the price of his wares.

"A bushel full of coins for each hide," he replied.

"You must be mad!" they all shouted at once. "Do you think we count money by the bushel?"

"Hides for sale! Hides for sale!" Big Claus repeated. And every time that someone asked him the price he said again, "A bushel full of coins."

"Are you trying to make fools of us?" the shoemakers and the tanners shouted. And while the crowd continued to gather around them, the tanners took their leather aprons and the shoemakers their straps and began to beat Big Claus.

"Hides . . . " screamed one of the tanners. "We'll see to it that your hide spits red!"

"Out of town with him!" they shouted. And certainly Big Claus did his best to get out of town as fast as he could; never in his whole life had he had such a beating.

"Little Claus is going to pay for this!" he decided when he got home. "He is going to pay with his life."

But while Big Claus was in town, something unfortunate had occurred: Little Claus's grandmother had died. And although she had been a very mean and scolding hag, who had never been kind to Little Claus, he felt very sad. Thinking that it might bring her back to life, he put his old grandmother in his own warm bed and decided to let her stay there all night, even though this meant that he would have to sleep in a chair.

It was not the first time that Little Claus had tried sleeping in a chair, but he could not sleep anyway; so he was wide awake when Big Claus came and tiptoed across the room to the bed in which he thought Little Claus was sleeping.

With an axe Big Claus hit the old grandmother on top of the head as hard as he could. "That's what you get for making a fool of me," he explained. "And now you won't be able to do it again," he added and went home.

"What a wicked man!" thought Little Claus. "If my grandmother hadn't already been dead, he would have killed her."

Very early the next morning he dressed his grandmother in her Sunday best; then he borrowed a horse from his neighbour and harnessed it to his cart. On the small seat in the back of the cart, he put the old woman in a sitting position with bundles on either side of her, so she wouldn't fall out of the cart while he was driving. He went through the forest and just as the sun was rising he reached an inn. "I'd better stop to get something to keep me alive," he said.

It was a large inn, and the innkeeper was very rich. He was also very kind, but he had a ferocious temper, as if he had nothing inside him but pepper and tobacco.

"Good morning," he said to Little Claus. "You're dressed very finely for so early in the morning."

"I'm driving to town with my grandmother," he replied. "She's sitting out in the cart because I couldn't persuade her to come in here with me. I wonder if you would be so kind as to take a glass of mead out to her; but speak a little loudly because she is a bit hard of hearing."

"No sooner said than done," answered the innkeeper; and he poured a large glass of mead which he carried out to the dead woman.

"Here is a glass of mead, which your son ordered for you," said the innkeeper loudly but politely; but the dead woman sat perfectly still and said not a word.

"Can't you hear me?" he shouted. "Here is mead from your son!"

He shouted the same words again as loud as he could, and still the old woman sat staring straight ahead. The more he shouted, the madder the innkeeper got, until finally he lost his temper and threw the mead, glass and all, right into the woman's face. With the mead dripping down her nose, she fell over backwards, for Little Claus had not tied her to the seat.

"What have you done?" shouted Little Claus as he flung open the door of the inn. "Why, you have killed my grandmother!" he cried, grabbing the innkeeper by the shirt. "Look at the wound she has on her head!"

"Oh, what a calamity!" the innkeeper exclaimed, and wrung his hands. "It is all because of that temper of mine! Sweet, good Little Claus, I will give you a bushel full of money and bury your grandmother as if she were my own, as long as you'll keep quiet about what really happened, because if you don't they'll chop my head off; and that's so nasty."

And that was how Little Claus got another bushel full of coins; and the innkeeper, true to his word, buried the old woman as well as he would have had she been his own grandmother.

As soon as he got home Little Claus sent his boy to borrow Big Claus's grain measure.

"What, haven't I killed him?" Big Claus exclaimed. "I must find out what's happened. I'll take the measure over there myself."

When he arrived at Little Claus's and saw all the money, his eyes grew wide with wonder and greed. "Where did you get all that from?" he demanded.

"It was my grandmother and not me that you killed, and now I have sold her body for a bushel full of money."

"You were certainly well paid," said Big Claus, and hurried home. When he got there he took an axe and killed his old grandmother; then he dumped the poor old woman's body in his carriage and drove into town. He went at once to the apothecary and asked if he wanted to buy a corpse.

"Who is it and where did you get it from?" the apothecary inquired.

"Oh, it is my grandmother, and I have killed her so I could sell her body for a bushel of money," Big Claus said.

"God save us!" cried the apothecary. "You don't know what you're saying . . . If you talk like that you'll lose your head." And the apothecary lectured him, telling him how wicked a crime murder was and that it was committed only by the most evil of men, who deserved the severest punishment. Big Claus was terrified and leaped into his carriage. He set off in the direction of his home, wildly whipping his horses. But no one tried to stop him, for everyone believed that he had gone mad.

"I'll make you pay for this!" Big Claus cried as soon as he was well out of town. "Little Claus is going to pay for this," he repeated when he got home. Then he took a large sack and went to see Little Claus.

"So you fooled me again!" he shouted. "First I killed my horses and then my grandmother; and it's all your fault. But you have fooled me for the last time!" Grabbing Little Claus around the waist, he shoved him into the sack. As he flung the sack over his shoulder he said loudly, "And now I am going to drown you!"

It was quite far to the river, and as he walked the sack with Little Claus in it seemed to grow heavier and heavier. The road went past the church, and Big Claus heard the organ being played and the congregation singing. "It would be nice to hear a hymn or two before I go on," he thought. "Everybody's in church and Little Claus can't get out of the sack." So Big Claus put down the sack near the entrance and went into the church.

"Poor me! Poor me!" sighed Little Claus. He twisted and turned but he could not loosen the cord that had been tied around the opening of the sack.

At that moment an old herdsman happened to pass. He had snow-white hair and as he walked, he leaned heavily on his long crook. In front of him he drove a large herd of cows and bulls. One of the bulls bumped into the sack and Little Claus was turned over.

"Poor me! Poor me!" cried Little Claus. "I am so young and am already bound for heaven."

"Think of poor me; I am an old man," said the herdsman, "and am not allowed to enter it."

"Open up the sack!" shouted Little Claus. "You get inside it, instead of me, and then you will get to heaven right away!"

"Nothing could be better," said the old man. He untied the sack and Little Claus crawled out at once.

"Take good care of my cattle," the herdsman begged as he climbed into the sack. Little Claus promised that he would and tied the sack securely. Then he went on his way, driving the herd before him.

A little later Big Claus came out of the church and lifted the sack on to his back. He was surprised how much lighter it was now, for the old man weighed only half as much as Little Claus.

"How easy it is to carry now; it did do me good to hear a hymn!" he thought.

Big Claus went directly down to the river that was both deep and wide and dumped the sack into the water, shouting after it: "You have made a fool of me for the last time!" For of course he believed that Little Claus was still inside the sack that was disappearing into the river.

On his way home he met Little Claus with all his cattle at the crossroads.

"What!" exclaimed Big Claus. "Haven't I drowned you?"

"Oh yes," answered Little Claus. "You threw me in the river about half an hour ago."

"But where did you get that huge herd of cattle?" Big Claus demanded.

"They are river cattle," replied Little Claus. "I'll tell you everything that happened to me. But, by the way, first I want to thank you for drowning me. For now I shall never have anything to worry about again, I am really rich. . . . Believe me, I was frightened when you threw me over the bridge. The wind whistled in my ears as I fell into the cold water. I sank straight to the bottom; but I didn't hurt myself because I landed on the softest, most beautiful green grass you can imagine. Then the sack was opened by the loveliest maiden. She was all dressed in white except for the green wreath in her wet hair. Taking my hand, she asked, 'Aren't you Little Claus?' When I nodded she said, 'Here are some cattle for you and six miles up the road there is an even bigger herd waiting for you.' Then I realized that to the water people the streams and rivers were as roads are to us. They use them to travel on. Far from their homes under the oceans, they follow the streams and the rivers until they finally become too shallow and come to an end. There are the most beautiful flowers growing down there and the finest, freshest grass; the fish swimming around above your head remind you of the birds flying in the air. The people are as nice as they can be; and the cattle fat and friendly."

"Then tell me why you came up here on land again?" asked Big Claus. "I never would have left a place as wonderful as that."

"Well," said Little Claus, "that is just because I am smart. I told you that the water maiden said that another herd of cattle would be waiting for me six miles up the road. By 'road,' she meant the river; and I am eager to see my cattle. You know how the river twists and turns while the road up here on land is straight; so I thought that if I used the road instead of the river I would get there much faster and save myself at least two miles of walking."

"Oh, you are a lucky man!" exclaimed Big Claus. "Do you think that if I were thrown into the river I would be given cattle too?"

"I don't know why not," replied Little Claus. "But I cannot carry you, as you did me, you're too heavy. But if you'll find a sack and climb into it yourself I'll be glad to go to the bridge with you and push you into the water."

"Thank you very much," said Big Claus. "But if I don't get a herd of cattle when I get down there I'll beat you as you have never been beaten before."

"Oh no! How can you think of being so cruel!" whimpered Little Claus as they made their way to the river.

It was a hot day and when the cattle spied the water they started running toward it, for they were very thirsty. "See how eager they are to get to the river," remarked Little Claus. "They are longing for their home under the water."

"Never mind them!" shouted Big Claus. "Or I'll give you a beating right here and now." He grabbed a sack that was lying on one of the bulls' backs and climbed up on the bridge. "Get a rock and put it in with me, I'm afraid that I might float."

"Don't worry about that," said Little Claus. But he found a big stone anyway and rolled it into the sack next to Big Claus before he tied the opening as tightly as he could. Then he pushed the sack off the bridge.

Splash! Plop! Down went Big Claus into the river and straight to the bottom he went.

"I am afraid that he will have trouble finding his cattle," said Little Claus, and drove his own herd home.

The Emperor's New Clothes

Many, many years ago there was an emperor who was so terribly fond of beautiful new clothes that he spent all his money on his attire. He did not care about his soldiers, or attending the theatre, or even going for a drive in the park, unless it was to show off his new clothes. He had an outfit for every hour of the day. And just as we say, "The king is in his council chamber," his subjects used to say, "The emperor is in his clothes closet."

In the large town where the emperor's palace was, life was gay and happy; and every day new visitors arrived. One day two swindlers came. They told everybody that they were weavers and that they could weave the most marvellous cloth. Not only were the colours and the patterns of their material extraordinarily beautiful, but the cloth had the strange quality of being invisible to anyone who was unfit for his office or unforgivably stupid.

"This is truly marvellous," thought the emperor. "Now if I had robes cut from that material, I should know which of my councillors was unfit for his office, and I would be able to pick out my clever subjects myself. They must weave some material for me!" And he gave the swindlers a lot of money so they could start working at once.

They set up a loom and acted as if they were weaving, but the loom was empty. The fine silk and gold threads they demanded from the emperor they never used, but hid them in their own knapsacks. Late into the night they would sit before their empty loom, pretending to weave.

"I would like to know how far they've come," thought the emperor; but his heart beat strangely when he remembered that those who were stupid or unfit for their office would not be able to see the material. Not that he was really worried that this would happen to him. Still, it might be better to send someone else the first time and see how he fared. Everybody in town had heard about the cloth's magic quality and most of them could hardly wait to find out how stupid or unworthy their neighbours were.

"I shall send my faithful prime minister to see the weavers," thought the emperor. "He will know how to judge the material, for he is both clever and fit for his office, if any man is."

The good-natured old man stepped into the room where the weavers were working and saw the empty loom. He closed his eyes, and opened them again. "God preserve me!" he thought. "I cannot see a thing!" But he didn't say it out loud.

The swindlers asked him to step a little closer so that he could admire the intricate patterns and marvellous colours of the material they were weaving. They both pointed to the empty loom, and the poor old prime minister opened his eyes as wide as he could; but it didn't help, he still couldn't see anything.

"Am I stupid?" he thought. "I can't believe it, but if it is so, it is best no one finds out about it. But maybe I am not fit for my office. No, that is worse, I'd better not admit that I can't see what they are weaving."

"Tell us what you think of it," demanded one of the swindlers.

"It is beautiful. It is very lovely," mumbled the old prime minister, adjusting his glasses. "What patterns! What colours! I shall tell the emperor that I am greatly pleased."

"And that pleases us," the weavers said; and now they described the patterns and told which shades of colour they had used. The prime minister listened attentively, so that he could repeat their words to the emperor; and that is exactly what he did.

The two swindlers demanded more money, and more silk and gold thread. They said they had to use it for their weaving, but their loom remained as empty as ever.

Soon the emperor sent another of his trusted councillors to see how the work was progressing. He looked and looked just as the prime minister had, but since there was nothing to be seen, he didn't see anything.

"Isn't it a marvellous piece of material?" asked one of the swindlers; and they both began to describe the beauty of their cloth again.

"I am not stupid," thought the emperor's councillor. "I must be unfit for my office. That is strange; but I'd better not admit it to anyone." And he started to praise the material, which he could not see, for the loveliness of its patterns and colours.

"I think it is the most charming piece of material I have ever seen," declared the councillor to the emperor.

Everyone in town was talking about the marvellous cloth that the swindlers were weaving.

At last the emperor himself decided to see it before it was removed from the loom. Attended by the most important people in the empire, among them the prime minister and the councillor who had been there before, the emperor entered the room where the weavers were weaving furiously on their empty loom.

"Isn't it *magnifique?*" asked the prime minister.

"Your Majesty, look at the colours and the patterns," said the councillor.

And the two old gentlemen pointed to the empty loom, believing that all the rest of the company could see the cloth.

"What!" thought the emperor. "I can't see a thing! Why, this is a disaster! Am I stupid? Am I unfit to be emperor? Oh, it is too horrible!" Aloud he said, "It is very lovely. It has my approval," while he nodded his head and looked at the empty loom.

All the councillors, ministers, and men of great importance who had come with him stared and stared; but they saw no more than the emperor had seen, and they said the same thing that he had said, "It is lovely." And they advised him to have clothes cut and sewn, so that he could wear them in the procession at the next great celebration.

"It is magnificent! Beautiful! Excellent!" All of their mouths agreed, though none of their eyes had seen anything. The two swindlers were decorated and given the title "Royal Knight of the Loom."

The night before the procession, the two swindlers didn't sleep at all. They had sixteen candles lighting up the room where they worked. Everyone could see how busy they were, getting the emperor's new clothes finished. They pretended to take the cloth from the loom; they cut the air with their big scissors, and sewed with needles without thread. At last they announced: "The emperor's clothes are ready!"

Together with his courtiers, the emperor came. The swindlers lifted their arms as if they were holding something in their hands, and said, "These are the trousers. This is the robe, and here is the train. They are all as light as if they were made of spider webs! It will be as if Your Majesty had almost nothing on, but that is their special virtue."

"Oh yes," breathed all the courtiers; but they saw nothing, for there was nothing to be seen.

"Will Your Imperial Majesty be so gracious as to take off your clothes?" asked the swindlers. "Over there by the big mirror, we shall help you put your new ones on."

The emperor did as he was told; and the swindlers acted as if they were dressing him in the clothes they should have made. Finally they tied around his waist the long train which two of his most noble courtiers were to carry.

The emperor stood in front of the mirror admiring the clothes he couldn't see.

"Oh, how they suit you! A perfect fit!" everyone exclaimed. "What colours! What patterns! The new clothes are magnificent!"

"The crimson canopy, under which Your Imperial Majesty is to walk, is waiting outside," said the imperial master of court ceremony.

"Well, I am dressed. Aren't my clothes becoming?" The emperor turned around once more in front of the mirror, pretending to study his finery.

The two gentlemen of the imperial bedchamber fumbled on the floor, trying to find the train which they were supposed to carry. They didn't dare admit that they didn't see anything, so they pretended to pick up the train and held their hands as if they were carrying it.

The emperor walked in the procession under his crimson canopy. And all the people of the town, who had lined the streets or were looking down from the windows, said that the emperor's new clothes were beautiful. "What a magnificient robe! And the train! How well the emperor's clothes suit him!"

None of them were willing to admit that they hadn't seen a thing; for if anyone did, then he was either stupid or unfit for the job he held. Never before had the emperor's clothes been such a success.

"But he doesn't have anything on!" cried a little child.

"Listen to the innocent one," said the proud father. And the people whispered among each other and repeated what the child had said.

"He doesn't have anything on. There's a little child who says that he has nothing on."

"He has nothing on!" shouted all the people at last.

The emperor shivered, for he was certain that they were right; but he thought, "I must bear it until the procession is over." And he walked even more proudly, and the two gentlemen of the imperial bedchamber went on carrying the train that wasn't there.

The Wild Swans

Far, far away where the swallows are when we have winter, there lived a king who had eleven sons and one daughter, Elisa. The eleven brothers were all princes; and when they went to school, each wore a star on his chest and a sword at his side. They wrote with diamond pencils on golden tablets, and read aloud so beautifully that everyone knew at once that they were of royal blood. Their sister Elisa sat on a little stool made of mirrors and had a picture book that had cost half the kingdom. How well those children lived; but it did not last.

Their father, who was king of the whole country, married an evil queen, and that boded no good for the poor children. They found this out the first day she came. The whole castle was decorated in honour of the great event, and the children decided to play house. Instead of the cakes and baked apples they usually were given for this game—and which were so easy to provide—the queen handed them a teacup full of sand and said that they should pretend it was something else.

A week later little Elisa was sent to live with some poor peasants; and the evil queen made the king believe such dreadful things about the princes that soon he did not care for them any more.

"Fly away, out into the world with you and fend for yourselves! Fly as voiceless birds!" cursed the queen; but their fate was not as terrible as she would have liked it to be, for her power had its limits. They became eleven beautiful, wild swans. With a strange cry, they flew out of the castle window and over the park and the forest.

It was very early in the morning when they flew over the farm where Elisa lived. She was still asleep in her little bed. They circled low above the roof of the farmhouse, turning and twisting their necks, to catch a glimpse of their sister, while their great wings beat the air. But no one was awake, and no one heard or saw them. At last they had to fly away, high up into the clouds, towards the great dark forest that stretched all the way to the ocean.

Poor little Elisa sat on the floor playing with a leaf. She had no toys, so she had made a hole in the leaf and was looking up at the sun through it. She felt as though she were looking into the bright eyes of her brothers; and when the warm sunbeams touched her cheeks, she thought of all the kisses they had given her.

The days passed, one after another, and they all were alike. The wind blew through the rosebush and whispered, "Who can be more lovely than you are?"

The roses shook their heads and replied: "Elisa!"

On Sundays the old woman at the farm would set her chair outside and sit reading her psalmbook. The wind would turn the leaves and whisper, "Who can be more saintly than you?"

The psalmbook would answer as truthfully as the roses had: "Elisa!"

When Elisa turned fifteen she was brought back to the castle. As soon as the evil queen saw how beautiful the girl was, envy and hate filled her evil heart. She would gladly have transformed Elisa into a swan at first sight; but the king had asked to see his daughter, and the queen did not dare to disobey him.

Early the next morning, before Elisa was awake, the queen went into the marble bathroom, where the floors were covered with costly carpets and the softest pillows lay on the benches that lined the walls. She had three toads with her. She kissed the first and said, "Sit on Elisa's head that she may become as lazy as you are." Kissing the second toad, she ordered, "Touch Elisa's forehead that she may become as ugly as you are, so her father will not recognize her." Then she kissed the third toad. "Rest next to Elisa's heart, that her soul may become as evil as yours and give her pain."

She dropped the toads into the clear water and, instantly, it had a greenish tinge. She sent for Elisa, undressed her, and told her to step into the bath. As she slipped into the water, the first toad leaped on to Elisa's head, the second touched her forehead, and the third snuggled as close to her heart as it could. But Elisa did not seem to notice them.

When Elisa rose from the bath, there floating on the water were three red poppies. If the toads had not been made poisonous by the kiss of the wicked queen, they would have turned into roses; but they had become flowers when they touched Elisa. She was so good and so innocent that evil magic could not harm her.

When the wicked queen realized this, she took the juice from walnut shells and rubbed Elisa's body till it was streaked black and brown; then she smeared an awful-smelling salve on the girl's face and filtered ashes and dust through her hair. Now it was impossible for anyone to recognize the lovely princess.

Her father got frightened when he saw her, and said, "She is not my daughter." Only the watchdog and the swallows recognized her; but they were only animals and nobody paid any attention to them.

Elisa wept bitterly and thought of her eleven brothers who had disappeared. In despair, she slipped out of the castle. She walked all day across fields and swamps until she came to the great forest. She did not know where she was going; she only knew that she was deeply unhappy and she longed more than ever to see her brothers again. She thought that they had been forced out into the world as she had; and now she would try to find them.

As soon as she entered the forest, night fell. She had come far away from any road or path. She lay down on the soft moss to sleep. She said her prayers and leaned her head against the stump of a tree. The night was silent, warm, and still. Around her shone so many glowworms that, when she touched the branch of a bush, the little insects fell to the ground like shooting stars.

That night she dreamed about her brothers. Again they were children writing on their golden tablets with diamond pens; and once more she looked at the lovely picture book that had cost half the kingdom. But on their tablets her brothers were not only doing their sums, they wrote of all the great deeds they had performed. The pictures in the book became alive: the birds sang, and the men and women walked right out of the book to talk to Elisa. Every time she was about to turn a leaf, they quickly jumped back on to the page, so as not to get in the wrong picture.

When she awoke, the sun was already high in the heavens; but she couldn't see it, for the forest was so dense that the branches of the tall trees locked out the sky. But the sun rays shone through the leaves and made a shimmering golden haze. The smell of greenness was all around her, and the birds were so tame that they almost seemed willing to perch on her shoulder. She heard the splashing of water; and she found a little brook, and followed it till it led her to a lovely little pool that was so clear, she could see the sand bottom in a glance. It was surrounded by bushes; but at one spot the deer, when they came down to drink, had made a hole. Here Elisa kneeled down.

Had the branches and their leaves not been swayed gently by the wind, she would have believed that they had been painted on the water, so perfectly were they mirrored. Those upon which the sun shone glistened, and those in the shade were a dark green.

Then Elisa saw her own face and was frightened: it was so dirty and ugly. She dipped her hand into the water and rubbed her eyes, her cheeks, and her forehead till she could see her own fresh skin again. She undressed and bathed in the clear pool, and a more beautiful princess than she, could not have been found in the whole world.

When she had dressed, braided her long hair, and drunk from the brook with her cupped hand, she wandered farther and farther into the forest without knowing where she was going. She thought about her brothers and trusted that God would not leave her. There ahead of her was a wild apple tree. Hadn't God let it grow there so that the hungry could eat? Its branches were bent almost to the ground under the weight of the fruit. Here Elisa rested and had her midday meal; before she walked on, she found sticks and propped up the heavily laden branches of the apple tree.

The forest grew darker and darker. It was so still that she could hear her own footsteps: the sound of every little stick, and leaf crumbling under her foot. No birds were to be seen or heard, no sunbeams penetrated the foliage. The trees grew so close together that when she looked ahead she felt as if she were imprisoned in a stockade. Oh, here she was more alone than she had ever thought one could be!

Night came and not a single glow-worm shone in the darkness. When she lay down to sleep she was hopelessly sad; but then the branches above her seemed to be drawn aside like a curtain, and she saw God looking down at her, with angels peeping over His shoulders and out from under His arms. And in the morning when she awoke, she did not know whether she had really seen God or it had merely been a dream.

Elisa met an old woman who was carrying a basket full of berries on her arm, and she offered the girl some berries. Elisa thanked her and then asked if she had seen eleven princes riding through the forest.

"No," the old woman replied. "But I have seen eleven swans with golden crowns on their heads, swimming in a stream not far from here."

She said she would show Elisa the way and led her to a cliff. Below it a little river twisted and turned its way through the forest. It seemed to be flowing in a tunnel, for the trees that grew on either side stretched their leafy branches towards each other and then intertwined. Where the branches were not long enough to span the stream, the trunks had pulled up part of their roots, in order to lean farther out over the water so the branches could meet.

Elisa said good-bye to the old woman and followed the stream until its water ran out into the sea.

Before her lay the beautiful ocean. There was not a sail to be seen nor any boat along the shore. She could not go any farther. How would she ever be able to find her brothers? She looked down. The shore was covered with pebbles: all the little stones were round; they had been made so by the sea. Iron, glass, stones, everything that lay at her feet had been ground into its present shape by water that was softer than her own delicate hand. "The waves roll on untiringly, and grind and polish the hardest stone. I must learn to be as untiring as they. Thank you for the lesson you have taught me, waves; and I am sure that one day you will carry me to my dear brothers."

Among the dried-out seaweed on the beach she found eleven swans' feathers. She picked them up; to each of them clung a drop of water, whether it was dew or a tear she did not know.

Although she was alone, Elisa did not feel lonely for she could watch the ever changing scene before her. The sea transforms itself more in an hour than a lake does in a year. When the clouds above it are dark, then the sea becomes as black as they are; and yet it will put on a dress of white if the wind should suddenly come and whip the waves. In the evening when the winds sleep and the clouds have turned pink, the sea will appear like the petal of a giant rose. Blue, white, green, red: the sea contains all colours; and even when it is calm, standing at the shore's edge, you will notice that it is moving like the breast of a sleeping child.

When the sun began to slide down behind the sea, Elisa saw eleven wild swans, with golden crowns on their heads, flying towards the beach. Like a white ribbon being pulled across the sky, they flew one after the other. Elisa hid behind some bushes. The swans landed nearby, still flapping their great white wings.

At the moment when the sun finally sank below the horizon, the swans turned into eleven handsome princes, Elisa's brothers. She shrieked with joy when she saw them. Although they had grown up since she had seen them last, she recognized them immediately and ran out from her hiding place to throw herself in their arms. They were as happy to see her as she was to see them. They laughed and cried, as they told each other of the evil deeds of their wicked stepmother.

"We must fly as wild swans as long as the sun is in the sky," explained the oldest brother. "Only when night has come do we regain our human shape; that is why we must never be in flight at sunset, for should we be up among the clouds, like any other human beings, we would fall and be killed. We do not live here, but in a country on the other side of the ocean. The sea is vast. It is far, far away; and there is no island where we can rest during our long journey. But midway in the ocean, a solitary rock rises above the waves. It is so tiny that we can just stand on it; and when the waves break against it, the water splashes up over us. Yet we thank God for that ragged rock, for if it were not there we should never be able to visit again the country where we were born. As it is, we only dare attempt the flight during the longest days of the year. We stay here eleven summer days and then we must return. Only for such a short time can we fly over the great forest and see our father's castle, and circle above the church where our mother is buried. It is as if every tree, every bush, in our native land were part of us. The wild horses gallop across the plains today as they did yesterday when we were children, and the gypsies still sing the songs we know. That is why we must come back—if only once a year. And now we have found you, our little sister. But we can only stay here two more days; then we must fly across the ocean to that fair land where we live now. How shall we be able to take you along? We have neither ship nor boat!"

"What can I do to break the spell that the queen has cast?" asked Elisa.

They talked almost the whole night through; only for a while did they doze. Elisa was awakened by the sound of wings beating the air. Her brothers had turned into swans again. They flew in circles above her and then disappeared over the forest. But her youngest brother had stayed behind. He rested his white head in her lap, and she stroked his strong

white wings. Just before sunset, the others returned; and when twilight came, they were princes once more.

"Tomorrow we must begin the flight back to our new homeland," said the oldest brother. "We dare not stay longer; but how can we leave you behind, Elisa? It will be a whole year before we can return. My arms when I am a man are strong enough to carry you through the forest; wouldn't the wings of all of us be strong enough to carry you over the sea when we are swans?"

"I'll go with you!" exclaimed Elisa.

They worked all night, weaving a net of reeds and willow branches. Just before sunrise, Elisa lay down upon it; and she was so tired that she fell asleep. When the sun rose, and the princes changed into swans again, they picked up the net with their bills and flew up into the clouds with their sleeping sister. The burning rays of the sun fell on her face, so one of the swans flew above her, to shade her with his great wings.

They were far out over the ocean when Elisa awoke. So strange did it feel to be carried through the air that at first she thought she was dreaming. Some berries and roots lay beside her. Her youngest brother had collected this provision for her journey, and it was he who now flew above her and shaded her from the sun.

The whole day they flew as swiftly as arrows through the air; yet their flight would have been even faster had they not been carrying Elisa. Soon the sun would begin to set. Dark clouds on the horizon warned of a coming storm. Elisa looked down; there was only the endless ocean; she saw no lonely rock. It seemed to her that the wings were beating harder now. She would be the cause of her brothers' deaths. When the sun set, they would turn into men again; then they would fall into the sea and be drowned. She prayed to God, but still there was no rocky islet to be seen. Black clouds filled the sky; soon the breath of the storm would be upon them. The waves seemed as heavy as lead, and in the clouds lightning flashed.

The rim of the sun touched the sea. Elisa trembled with fear. Suddenly the swans dived down so fast that she thought that they were falling; but then they spread out their wings again.

Half of the sun had disappeared when Elisa saw the little rock. Looking down from the air, she thought that it looked more like a seal who had raised his head above the water. Just as the sun vanished they landed on the rock; and when the last of its light, like a piece of paper set aflame, flared up and then was gone, her brothers stood around her arm in arm.

The island was so tiny that they had to stand holding on to each other all night. The lightning made the sky bright and the thunder roared. They held each other's hands and sang a psalm, which comforted them and gave them courage.

At dawn the storm was over and the air was fresh and clear. The swans flew away from the rock, carrying Elisa. The sea was still turbulent. The white surf looked like millions of swans swimming on a raging green ocean. When the sun was high in the sky, Elisa saw a strange landscape. There was a mountain range covered with ice and snow. Halfway down the mountainsides was a huge palace, miles long, made of arcades, one on top of the other. And below that was a forest of gently waving palm trees, in which there were flowers with faces as large as millstones. She asked if that were the country where they lived, and the swans shook their heads. What she was seeing was a fata morgana: a mirage, an ever changing castle in the air to which no human being could gain admittance. As Elisa stared at it, the mountains, the castle, and the forest disappeared. It melted together and now there were twenty proud churches, every one alike, with high towers and tall windows. She thought she heard their organs playing, but it was the sound of the sea beating far below. The churches, in turn, changed into ships with towering sails. She was just above them; but when she looked down, she saw only fog driven by wind over the waves. The world of the sea and the air is always changing, ever in motion.

At last she saw the shores of the real country that was their destination. The mountains, which were covered with forests of cedar, were blue in the afternoon light; and she could see castles and towns. Before the sun had set, the swans alighted in front of a cave; its walls were covered with vines and plants that had intertwined and looked like tapestries.

"Tomorrow you must tell us what you have dreamed," said her youngest brother, showing her the part of the cave that was to be her bedchamber.

"May I dream how I can break the spell that the wicked queen cast," she said fervently; and that thought absorbed her so completely that she prayed to God and begged Him to help her; and while she was falling asleep she kept on praying.

Elisa felt as though she were flying into the fata morgana, the castle in the air; and a fairy came to welcome her who was young and beautiful, and yet somehow resembled the old woman whom Elisa had met in the forest and who had told her about the eleven swans with golden crowns on their heads.

"Your brothers can escape their fate," began the fairy, "if you have enough courage and endurance. The waves of the ocean are softer than your hands, yet they can form and shape hard stones; but they cannot feel the pain that your fingers will feel. They have no hearts and therefore they do not know fear: the suffering that you must endure. Look at the nettle that I hold in my hand! Around the cave where you are sleeping grow many of them; only those nettles or the ones to be found in churchyards may you use. You must pick them, even though they blister and burn your hands; then you must stamp on them with your bare feet until they become like flax. And from that you must twine thread with which to knit eleven shirts with long sleeves. If you cast one of these shirts over each of the eleven swans, the spell will be broken. But remember, from the moment you start your work until it is finished, you must be silent and never speak to anyone—even if it takes you years, you must be mute! If you speak one word, that word will send a knife into the hearts of your brothers. Their lives depend on your tongue: remember!"

The fairy touched Elisa's hand with the nettle. It felt like fire and she woke. It was bright daylight. Near her lay a nettle like the one she had seen in her sleep. She fell on her knees and said a prayer of thanks; then she walked outside to begin her work.

Her delicate hands picked the horrible nettles, and it felt as if her hands were burning and big blisters rose on her arms and hands. But she did not mind the pain if she could save her brothers. She broke every nettle and stamped on it with her bare feet until it became as fine as flax and could be twined into green thread.

When the sun set, her brothers came. At first they feared that some spell had been cast upon their sister by their evil stepmother, for Elisa was silent and would not answer their questions. But when they saw her hands covered with blisters, they understood the work she was doing was for their sake. The youngest of her brothers cried and his tears fell on her hands; the pain ceased and the burning blisters disappeared.

That night she could not sleep; she worked the whole night through. She felt that she could not rest until her brothers were free. The following day she was alone, but time passed more swiftly. By sunset the first of the nettle shirts was finished.

The next day she heard the sound of hunters' horns coming from the moutains. They came nearer and nearer and soon she could hear dogs barking. Frightened, she bound the nettles she had collected into a bundle with the thread she had already twined and the finished shirt; then she fled into the cave and sat down on the nettle heap.

Out of the thicket sprang a large dog; then came another and another. Barking, they ran back and forth in front of the entrance to the cave. Within a few minutes the hunters followed. The handsomest among them was the king of the country. He entered the cave and found Elisa. Never before had he seen a girl lovelier than she.

"Why are you hiding here, beautiful child?" he asked. Elisa shook her head. She dared not speak because her brothers' lives depended upon her silence. She hid her hands behind her back so that the king might not see how she suffered.

"You cannot stay here," he said. "Follow me, and if you are as good as you are beautiful, then you shall be clad in velvet and silk, wear a golden crown on your head, and call the loveliest of my castles your home."

He lifted her up on his horse. Elisa cried and wrung her hands. The king would not set her down again. "I only want to make you happy," he said. "Someday you will thank me for what I have done." Then he spurred his horse and galloped away with Elisa. The other hunters followed him.

By evening they reached the royal city with its many churches and palaces. The king led her into his castle with its lofty halls, where the waters of the fountains splashed into marble basins, and where the ceilings and the walls were beautifully painted. But none of this did Elisa notice, for she was crying so sorrowfully, so bitterly.

Silently but good-naturedly, she let the maids dress her in regal gowns, braid her hair with pearls, and pull long gloves over her blistered hands. When she entered the great hall, dressed so magnificently, she was so beautiful that the whole court bowed and curtsied. The king declared that she was to be his queen. Only the archbishop shook his head and whispered that he believed the little forest girl to be a witch who had cast a spell over the king.

The king did not listen to him. He ordered the musicians to play and the feast to begin. Dancing girls danced for Elisa; and the king showed her the fragrant gardens and the grand halls of his castle. But neither her lips nor her eyes smiled. Sorrow had printed its eternal mark on her face. Finally the king showed her a little chamber. Its walls and floor were covered by costly green carpets. It looked like the cave where she had been with her brothers. In a corner lay the green thread which she had spun from the nettles, and from the ceiling hung the one shirt that she had already knitted. One of the hunters had taken it all along as a curiosity.

"Here you can dream yourself back to your former home," remarked the king. "Here is the work you used to do; it will amuse you amid present splendour to think of the past."

A sweet smile played for a moment on Elisa's lips when she saw what was nearest and dearest to her heart restored to her. The colour returned to her cheeks. She thought of her brothers, and she kissed the king's hand. He pressed her to his breast and ordered that all the church bells be rung and their wedding proclaimed. The silent girl from the woods was to become the queen.

The archbishop whispered evil words in the king's ear, but they did not penetrate his heart. The marriage ceremony was held, and the archbishop himself had to crown the queen. He pressed the golden band down on her head so hard that it hurt. But she did not feel the pain, for sorrow's band squeezed her heart and made her suffer far more.

She must not speak a word or her brothers would die. But her eyes spoke silently of the love she felt for the king, who did everything he could to please her. Every day she loved him more. If only she could tell him of her anguish. But mute she must be until her task was finished. At night while the king slept, she would leave their bed and go to the chamber with the green carpets, and make the nettle shirts for her brothers. But when she had finished the sixth shirt she had no more green thread with which to knit.

She knew that in the churchyard grew the nettles that she needed. She had to pick them herself. But how was she to go there without anyone seeing her?

"What is the pain in my hands compared to the pain I feel in my heart?" she thought. "I must attempt it and God will help me."

As if it were an evil deed she was about to perform, she sneaked fearfully out of the castle late at night. She crossed the royal park and made her way through the empty streets to the churchyard. The moon was out; and on one of the large tombstones she saw a group of lamias sitting. They are those dreadful monsters with the bodies of snakes and the breasts and heads of women. They dig up the graves of those who have just died, to eat the flesh of the corpses. Elisa had to walk past them. She said her prayers, and though they kept their terrible gaze upon her, they did her no harm. She picked her nettles and returned to the castle.

Only one person had seen her: the archbishop, for he was awake when everyone else was sleeping. Now he thought that what he had said was proven true: the queen was a witch who had cast her spell on the king and all his subjects.

When next the king came to confession, the archbishop told him what he had seen and what he feared. He spoke his condemning words so harshly that the carved sculptures of the saints shook their heads as though they were saying: "It is not true. Elisa is innocent!"

But that was not the way the archbishop interpreted it; he said that the saints were shaking their heads because of their horror at her sins.

Two tears rolled down the king's cheeks, and with a heavy heart he returned to the castle. That night he only pretended to sleep and, when Elisa rose, he followed her. Every night she went on with her work; and every night the king watched her disappear into the little chamber.

The face of the king grew dark and troubled. Elisa noticed it, though she did not know its cause; and this new sorrow was added to her fear for her brothers' fate. On her royal velvet dress fell salt tears, and they looked like diamonds on the purple material, making it even more splendid. And all the women of the court wished that they were queens and could wear such magnificient clothes.

Soon Elisa's work would be over. She had to knit only one more shirt; but she had no more nettles from which to twine thread. Once more, for the last time, she would have to go to the churchyard. She shook with fear when she thought of walking alone past the horrible lamias, but she gathered courage when she thought of her brothers and her own faith in God.

Elisa went; and secretly the king and the archbishop followed her. They saw her disappear through the gates of the churchyard. The same terrifying lamias were there, and they were sitting near the place where the nettles grew. The king saw her walk toward them, and he turned away as his heart filled with repulsion, for he thought that Elisa, his queen — who that very night had rested in his arms — had come to seek the company of these monsters.

"Let the people judge her," said he. And the people judged her guilty and condemned her to the stake.

She was taken from the great halls of the castle and thrown into a dungeon, when the wind whistled through the grating that barred the window. Instead of a bed with silken sheets and velvet pillows, they gave her the nettles she had picked as a pillow and the shirts she had knitted as a cover. They could have given her no greater gift. She prayed to God and started work on the last of the shirts. Outside in the streets, the urchins sang songs that mocked and scorned her, while no one said a word of comfort to her.

Just before sunset, she heard the sound of swan's wings beating before her window. It was her youngest brother who had found her. She wept for happiness, even though she knew that this might be the last night of her life. Her work was almost done and her brothers were near her.

The archbishop had promised the king that he would be with Elisa during the last hours of her life. But when he came, she shook her head and pointed towards the door, to tell him to go. Her work must be finished that night or all her suffering, all her tears, all her pain would be in vain. The archbishop spoke some unkind words to her and left.

Poor Elisa, who knew that she was innocent but could not say a word to prove it, set to work knitting the last shirt. Mice ran across the floor and fetched the nettles for her; they wanted to help. And the thrush sang outside the iron bars of the window, as gaily as it could, so that she would not lose her courage.

One hour before sunrise, her brothers came to the castle and demanded to see the king. But they were refused, for it was still night and the guards did not dare wake the king. Elisa's brothers begged and threatened; they made so much noise that the captain of the guard came and, finally, the king himself. But at that moment the sun rose; the brothers were gone but high above the royal castle flew eleven white swans.

A stream of people rushed through the gates of the city. Everyone wanted to see the witch being burned. An old worn-out mare drew the cart in which Elisa sat. She was clad in sackcloth; her hair hung loose and framed her beautiful face, which was deadly pale. Her lips moved; she was mumbling a prayer while she knitted the last shirt. The other ten lay at her feet. Even on the way to her death she did not cease working. The mob that lined the road jeered and mocked her.

"Look at the witch, she is mumbling her spells!" they screamed. "See what she has in her hands! It is no hymnbook; it is witchcraft! Get it away from her and tear it into a thousand pieces!"

And the rabble tried to stop the cart and tear Elisa's knitting out of her hands. But at that moment eleven white swans flew down and perched on the railing of the cart; they beat the air with their strong wings. The people drew back in fear.

"It is a sign from heaven that she is innocent," some of them whispered; but not one of them dared say it aloud.

The executioner took her hand to lead her to the stake, but she freed herself from him, grabbed the eleven shirts, and cast them over the swans. There stood eleven princes, handsome and fair. But the youngest of them had a swan's wing instead of an arm, for Elisa had not been able to finish one of the sleeves of the last shirt.

"Now I dare speak!" she cried. "I am innocent!"

The people, knowing that a miracle had taken place, kneeled down before her as they would have for a saint. But Elisa, worn out by fear, worry, and pain, fainted lifelessly into the arms of one of her brothers.

"Yes, she is innocent!" cried the oldest brother; and he addressed himself to the king and told of all that had happened to himself, his brothers, and their sister Elisa. While he spoke a fragrance of millions of roses spread from the wood that had been piled high around the stake. Every stick, every log had taken root and set forth vines. They were a hedge of the loveliest red roses, and on the very top bloomed a single white rose. It shone like a star. The king plucked it and placed it on Elisa's breast. She woke; happiness and peace were within her.

The church bells in the city started to peal, though no bell ringers pulled their ropes, and great flocks of birds flew in the sky. No one has ever seen a gayer procession than the one that now made its way to the royal castle.

The Old House

Once upon a time there stood in a street a very old house; it was nearly three hundred years old. You could tell what year it had been built by reading the date cut into one of the beams; all around it tulips and curling hop vines had been carved. Right above the entrance a whole verse had been inscribed, and above each window appeared a grinning face. The second storey protruded over the first. The lead gutters, which hung under the roof, were shaped like dragons, with the monster's head at either end. The water was supposed to spout out of their mouths, but it didn't; the gutter was filled with holes and the water ran out of the dragons' stomachs.

All the other houses in the street were new and well kept, their walls were straight and smooth, and they had large windows. It was quite reasonable that they should feel themselves superior to the old house. Had they been able to speak they probably would have said: "How long are we to tolerate that old ruin? Bow windows are out of fashion and, besides, they obstruct our view. It must believe itself to be a castle, judging from the size of the steps leading up to the entrance, and that iron railing makes one think of funerals; not to speak of the brass knobs. It's embarrassing!"

Right across from the old house stood a new house; it was of the same opinion as all the other houses in the street. But behind one of its windows sat a little boy, a little red-cheeked child with bright, shining eyes who preferred the old house, and that both in the daytime when the sun shone and at night in the moonlight. When he looked at the walls of the old house, with its cracks and bare spots where the mortar had fallen off, then he could imagine how the street once had looked: in olden times, when all the houses had had broad steps leading up to their doors, and bay windows, and gables with tall pointed roofs. He could see the soldiers marching through the streets armed with halberds. Oh, he found the old house worth looking at and dreaming about.

Its owner was an old man who wore the strangest old-fashioned breeches, a coat with brass buttons, and a wig that you could see was a wig. Every morning an old servant arrived to clean and run errands for the old gentleman; otherwise, he was all alone. Sometimes he came to the window and looked out into the street; then the little boy nodded to him and the old man nodded back. In this manner they became acquainted; no, more than that, they were friends, although they had never spoken to each other.

The little boy heard his parents say, "Our neighbour, across the street, must be terribly lonely."

Next Sunday the boy made a little package and, when he saw the servant going by in the street, he hurried down and gave it to him. "Would you please give this to your master?" he asked. "I have two tin soldiers, and I would like your master to have one of them, for I have heard that he is so terribly lonely."

The old servant smiled and nodded and took the little package, with the tin soldier inside it, to his master. Later that day a message arrived, inviting the boy to come and visit the old man. The child's parents gave their permission; and thus he finally entered the old house.

The brass knobs on the iron railing seemed to shine so brightly that one might believe that they had been newly polished in honour of the boy's visit. The little carved trumpeters in the oak doorway seemed to be blowing especially hard on their instruments, for their cheeks were all puffed up. It was a fanfare! "Tra . . . tra . . trattalala! The boy is coming! Tra . . . tra . . trattalala!" The door was opened and he stood in the hall. All the walls were covered with paintings portraying ladies in long silk gowns and knights in armour. The boy thought that he could hear the silk gowns rustle and the armour clang. Then there were the stairs; first they went up a goodish way, and then down a little bit, and ended in a balcony. It was wooden and a bit rickety, grass and weeds grew out of every crack, making it look more like a garden than a balcony. Antique flowerpots with human faces and donkey ears stood ranged in a row; the plants grew to suit themselves. One of them was filled with carnations that spread out over the rim in all directions; that is, the green leaves and the stems, the flowers hadn't come yet. One could almost hear the plant saying: "The breeze has caressed me and the sun has kissed me and promised me a flower next Sunday, a little flower next Sunday."

The old servant led the boy into a chamber where the walls did not have paper on them; no, they were covered with leather, which had gilded flowers stamped upon it.

> *"Gilding fades all too fast.*
> *Leather, that is meant to last,"*

said the walls.

In the room were high-backed armchairs with carvings all over them. "Sit down, sit down!" they cried. And when you sat down in them they mumbled. "Ugh, how it cracks inside me! I think I've got rheumatism like the old cabinet. Ugh, how it creaks and cracks."

At last the little boy entered the room with the bow windows. Here the old master of the house greeted him. "Thank you for the tin soldier, my little friend," said he. "And thank you for coming."

"Thanks, thanks," said all the furniture, although it sounded a little more like: "Crack . . . Crack." There were so many chairs, tables, and cabinets in the room that they stood in each other's way, for they all wanted to see the little boy at once.

In the centre of one of the walls hung a picture of a beautiful young girl. She was laughing and dressed in clothes from a bygone time. She did not say "thank you" or "crack" as the furniture had, but she looked down so kindly at the little boy that he could not help asking, "Where did you get her?"

"From the pawnbroker's," replied the old gentleman. "His shop is filled with pictures that no one cares about any more. The people they portray have been dead so long that no one remembers them. But though she has been dead and gone for fifty years, I knew her once."

Under the portrait hung a bouquet of faded flowers, carefully preserved behind glass. They looked old enough to have been picked half a century ago. The pendulum of the grandfather clock swung back and

forth, and the hands moved slowly around, telling everything in the room that time was passing and that they were getting older; but that did not disturb the furniture.

"My parents say that you are terribly lonely," said the little boy.

"Oh," the old man smiled, "that is not altogether true. Old thoughts, old dreams, old memories come and visit me and now you are here. I am not unhappy."

Then from a shelf he took down a book that was filled with wonderful pictures. There were processions in which there were golden carriages, knights, and kings who looked like the ones in a deck of cards; and then came the citizens carrying the banners of their trades: the tailors' emblem was a pair of scissors held by a lion; the shoemakers had an eagle with two heads above their banner—for, as you know, shoemakers do everything in pairs. What a picture book that was!

The old man left for a moment to fetch some comfits, apples, and nuts; it was certainly nice to be visiting the old house.

"But I can't stand it here!" wailed the tin soldier, who was standing on the lid of a chest. "It is so lonely and sad here; once you have lived with a family you cannot get accustomed to being alone. I can't stand it! The days are so long and the evenings feel even longer. It is not the same here as in your home, where your parents talked so pleasantly and you sweet children made such a lot of lovely noise. No, that poor old man really is lonely. Do you think anybody ever gives him a kiss? Or looks kindly at him? Here there is no Christmas tree ever, or gifts! The only thing he will ever get will be a funeral! . . . I can't stand it!"

"You mustn't take it so to heart," said the little boy. "I think it is very nice here. All the old thoughts and dreams come to visit him, so he said."

"I see none of them and I don't want to either," screamed the tin soldier. "I can't stand it!"

"You will have to," said the little boy just as the old man returned with the comfits, apples, and nuts; and at the sight of them the boy forgot all about the soldier.

Happy and content, the little boy returned home. Days and weeks went by. The boy nodded to the old man from his window, and from the funny bow window of the old house the greeting was returned. Finally the little boy was asked to come visiting again.

The carved trumpeters blew, "Tra . . . tra . . . tratralala. . . . The boy is here! . . . Tra tra!" The knights in armour clanged with their swords and the silk gowns of the ladies rustled, the leather on the wall said its little verse, and the old chairs that had rheumatism creaked. Nothing had changed, for in the old house every day and hour were exactly alike.

"I can't stand it!" screamed the tin soldier as soon as he saw the boy. "I have wept tin tears! It is much too mournful and sad here. Please, let me go to the wars and lose my arms and legs, that at least will be a change. I can't stand it, for I know what it is like to have old thoughts and old memories come visiting. Mine have been here and that is not amusing. Why, I almost jumped right off the lid of the chest. I saw all of you and my own home as plainly as if I had been there. It was Sunday morning and all you children were standing around the big table singing hymns, as you always do on Sunday. Your parents were nearby, looking solemn. Suddenly the door opened and little Maria, who is only two years old, entered. She always dances whenever she hears music, and she tried to dance to the tune you were singing, but hymns are not made for dancing they are too slow. She stood first on one leg and flung her head forward, and then on the other and flung her head forward, but it didn't work out. You looked grave, all of you, but I found it too difficult not to laugh—at least inside myself. I laughed so hard that I fell off the table and hit my head so hard that I got a lump on it. I know it was wrong of me to laugh and the lump was punishment for it. That is what the old man meant by old thoughts and memories: everything that has ever happened to you comes back inside you. . . . Tell me, do you still sing your hymns on Sunday? Tell me something about little Maria and about my comrade, the other tin soldier. He must be happy. Oh, I can't stand it!"

"I have given you away," said the little boy. "You will have to stay, can't you understand that?"

The old man brought him a drawer in which lay many wonderful things. There were old playing cards with gilded edges, a little silver piggy bank, and a fish with a wiggly tail. Other drawers were opened and all the curiosities were looked at and examined. Finally the old man opened the harpsichord; on the inside of the lid was a painting of a landscape. The instrument was out of tune but the old man played on it anyway, and hummed a melody.

"Ah yes, she used to sing that," he sighed, and looked up towards the painting he had bought from the pawnbroker and his eyes shone like a young man's.

"I am going to the wars! I am going to the wars!" screamed the tin

145

soldier as loudly as he could, and fell off the chest.

"What could have happened to him?" said the old man. Together he and the boy were searching for the little soldier on the floor. "Never mind, I will find him later," said the old man, but he never did. There were so many cracks in the floor and the tin soldier had fallen right down through one of them; there he lay buried alive.

The day passed and the little boy returned home. Many weeks went by, winter had come. All the windows were frozen over. The little boy had to breathe on the glass until he could thaw a little hole so that he could see out. Across the street the old house looked quite deserted; the snow lay in drifts on the steps. They had not been swept; one would think no one was at home. And no one was. The kind old man had died.

That evening a hearse drew up in front of the old house and a coffin was carried down the steps. The old man was not to be buried in the town cemetery but somewhere out in the country, where he had been born. The hearse drove away. No one followed it, for all his friends and family had died long ago. The little boy kissed his fingers and threw a kiss after the hearse as it disappeared down the street.

A few days afterwards an auction was held; the furniture in the old house was sold. The boy watched from the window. He saw the knights in armour and the ladies with their silken gowns being carried out of the house. The old high-backed chairs, the funny flowerpots with faces and donkey ears were bought by strangers. Only the portrait of the lady found no buyer; it was returned to the pawnbroker. There it hung; no one remembered her and no one cared for the old picture.

Next spring the house itself was torn down, "It was a monstrosity," said the people as they went by. One could see right into the room with the leather-covered walls; the leather was torn and hung flapping like banners in the wind. The grass and weeds on the balcony clung tenaciously to the broken beams. But at last all was cleared away.

"That was good," said the neighbouring houses.

A new house was built, with straight walls and big windows but not quite where the old house had stood; it was a little farther back from the street. On the site of the old house a little garden was planted, and up the walls of the houses on either side grew vines. A fine iron fence with a gate enclosed it, and people would stop in the street to look in, for it was most attractive. The sparrows would sit in the vines and talk and talk as sparrows do, but not about the old house, for they were too young to remember it.

Years went by and the little boy had become a grown man, a good and clever man of whom his parents could be justly proud. He had just got married and had moved into the new house. His young wife was planting a little wild flower in the front garden. He was watching her with a smile. Just as she finished, and was patting the earth around the little plant, she pricked her little hand. Something sharp was sticking out of the soft earth. What could it be?

It was—imagine it!—the tin soldier! The one that had fallen off the chest and down through a crack in the flooring. It had survived the wrecking of the old house, falling hither and thither as beams and floors disappeared, until at last it had been buried in the earth and there it had lain for many years.

The young woman cleaned the soldier off with a green leaf and then with her own handkerchief. It had perfume on it and smelled so delicious that the soldier felt as though he were awakening from a deep sleep.

"Let me have a look at him," said the young man; then he laughed and shook his head. "I don't believe it can be him, but he reminds me of a tin soldier that I once had." Then he told his wife about the old house and its old master and about the tin soldier that he had sent over to keep the old man company, when he had been a boy, because he had known that the old man was so terribly alone.

He told the story so well that his young wife's eyes filled with tears as she heard about the old house and the old man. "It could be the same soldier," she said. "I will keep it so that I shall not forget the story you have told me. But you must show me the old man's grave."

"I do not know where it is," her husband replied. "No one does; all those who knew him were dead. You must remember that I was a very small boy then."

"How terribly lonely he must have been," sighed the young woman.

"Yes, terribly lonely," echoed the tin soldier. "But it is truly good to find that one is not forgotten."

"Good," croaked something nearby in so weak a voice that only the tin soldier heard it. It was a little piece of leather from the walls of the old house. The gilding had gone long ago, and it looked like a little clod of wet earth. But it still had an opinion, and it expressed it.

"Gilding fades all too fast,
But leather, that is meant to last."

But the tin soldier did not believe that.

The Little Mermaid

Far, far from land, where the waters are as blue as the petals of the cornflower and as clear as glass, there, where no anchor can reach the bottom, live the mer-people. So deep is this part of the sea that you would have to pile many church towers on top of each other before one of them emerged above the surface.

Now you must not think that at the bottom of the sea there is only white sand. No, here grow the strangest plants and trees; their stems and leaves are so subtle that the slightest current in the water makes them move, as if they were alive. Big and small fishes flit in and out among their branches, just as the birds do up on earth. At the very deepest place, the mer-king has built his castle. Its walls are made of coral and its long pointed windows of amber. The roof is oyster shells that are continually opening and closing. It looks very beautiful, for in each shell lies a pearl, so lustrous that it would be fit for a queen's crown.

The mer-king had been a widower for many years; his mother kept house for him. She was a very intelligent woman but a little too proud of her rank; she wore twelve oysters on her tail; the nobility were only allowed six. Otherwise, she was a most praiseworthy woman, and she took excellent care of her grandchildren, the little princesses. They were six lovely mermaids; the youngest was the most beautiful. Her complexion was as fine as the petal of a rose and her eyes as blue as the deepest lake but, just like everyone else down there, she had no feet; her body ended in a fishtail.

The mermaids were allowed to play all day in the great hall of the castle, where flowers grew on the walls. The big amber windows were kept open and the fishes swam in and out, just as the swallows up on earth fly in through our windows if they are open. But unlike the birds of the air, the fishes were not frightened, they swam right up to the little princesses and ate out of their hands and let themselves be petted.

Around the castle was a great park where there grew fiery-red and deep-blue trees. Their fruits shone as though they were the purest gold, their flowers were like flames, and their branches and leaves were ever in motion. The earth was the finest sand, not white but blue, the colour of burning sulphur. There was a blue tinge to everything, down on the bottom of the sea. You could almost believe that you were suspended in mid-air and had the blue sky both above and below you. When the sea was calm, the sun appeared like a crimson flower, from which all light flowed.

Each little princess had her own garden, where she could plant the flowers she liked. One of them had shaped her flower bed so it resembled a whale; and another, as a mermaid. The youngest had planted red flowers in hers: she wanted it to look like the sun; it was round and the crimson flowers did glow as though they were so many little suns. She was a strange little child: quiet and thoughtful. Her sisters' gardens were filled with all sorts of things that they had collected from shipwrecks, but she had only a marble statue of a boy in hers. It had been cut out of stone that was almost transparently clear and had sunk to the bottom of the sea when the ship that had carried it was lost. Close to the statue she had planted a pink tree; it looked like a weeping willow. The tree was taller than the sculpture. Its long soft branches bent towards the sand; it looked as if the top of the tree and its roots wanted to kiss each other.

The princesses liked nothing better than to listen to their old grandmother tell about the world above. She had to recount countless times all she knew about ships, towns, human beings, and the animals that lived up on land. The youngest of the mermaids thought it particularly wonderful that the flowers up there had fragrance, for that they did not have on the bottom of the sea. She also liked to hear about the green forest, where the fishes that swam among the branches could sing most beautifully. Grandmother called the birds "fishes"; otherwise, her little grandchildren would not have understood her, since they had never seen a bird.

"But when you are fifteen, then you will be allowed to swim to the surface," she promised. "Then you can climb up on a rock and sit and watch the big ships sail by. If you dare, you can swim close enough to the shore to see the towns and the forest."

The following year, the oldest of the princesses would be fifteen. From one sister to the next, there was a difference in age of about a year, which meant that the youngest would have to wait more than five whole years before she would be allowed to swim up from the bottom of the sea and take a look at us. But each promised the others that she would return after her first day above, and tell about the things she had seen and describe what she thought was loveliest of all. For the old grandmother could not satisfy their curiosity.

None of the sisters longed so much to see the world above as the youngest, the one who had to wait the longest before she could leave her home. Many a night this quiet, thoughtful little mermaid would stand by the open window, looking up through the dark blue waters where the fishes swam. She could see the moon and the stars; they looked paler but larger down here under the sea. Sometimes a great shadow passed by like a cloud and then she knew that it was either a whale or a ship, with its crew and passengers, that was sailing high above her. None on board could have imagined that a little beautiful mermaid stood in the depths below them and stretched her little white hands up towards the keel of their ship.

The oldest of the sisters had her fifteenth birthday and swam up to the surface of the sea. When she returned she had hundreds of things to tell. But of everything that had happened to her, the loveliest experience by far, she claimed, had been to lie on a sandbank, when the sea was calm and the moon was out, and look at a great city. The lights from the windows and streets had shone like hundreds of stars; and she had been able to hear the rumbling of the carriages and the voices of human beings and, best of all, the sound of music. She had seen all the church towers and steeples and heard their bells ring. And just because she would never be able to enter the city, she longed to do that more than anything else.

How carefully her youngest sister listened to every word and remembered everything that she had been told. When, late in the evening, the little mermaid would stand dreaming by the window and look up through the blue water, then she imagined that she could see the city and hear the bells of the churches ringing.

The next year the second of the sisters was allowed to swim away from home. Her little head had emerged above the water just at the moment when the sun was setting. This sight had been so beautiful that she could hardly describe it. The whole heaven had been covered in gold and the clouds that had sailed above her had been purple and crimson. A flight of wild swans, like a white veil just above the water, had flown by. She had swum toward the sun, but it had set, taking the colours of the clouds, sea, and sky with it.

The third of the sisters, who came of age the following year, was the most daring among them. She had swum way up a broad river! There she had seen green hills covered with vineyards, castles, and farms that peeped out through the great forests. She had heard the birds sing and the sun had been so hot that she had had to swim under the water, some of the time, just to cool off. In a little bay, she had come upon some naked children who were playing and splashing in the water. She had wanted to join them, but when they saw her they got frightened and ran away. A little black animal had come: it was a dog. But she had never seen one before. It had barked so loudly and fiercely that she became terrified and swam right back to the sea. What she never would forget as long as she lived were the beautiful forest, the green hills, and the sweet little children who had been able to swim even though they had no fishtails as she had.

The fourth of the sisters was timid. She stayed far away from shore, out in the middle of the ocean. But that was the most beautiful place of all, she asserted. You could see far and the sky above was like a clear glass bell. The ships she had seen had been so far away that they had looked no bigger than gulls. But the little dolphins had turned somersaults for her and the great whales had sprayed water high up into the air, so that it looked as though there were more than a hundred fountains.

The fifth sister's birthday was in the winter and, therefore, she saw something none of her sisters had seen. The ocean had been green, and huge icebergs had been floating on it. Each of them had been as lovely as a pearl and yet larger than the church towers that human beings built. They had the most fantastic shapes and their surface glittered like diamonds. She had climbed up on the largest one of them all; the wind had played with her long hair, and all the ships had fearfully kept away. Toward evening a storm had begun to blow; dark clouds had gathered and bolts of lightning had flashed while the thunder rolled. The waves had lifted the iceberg high up on their shoulders, and the lightning had coloured the ice red. The ships had taken down their sails; and on board, fear and terror had reigned. But the mermaid had just sat on her iceberg and watched the bolts of lightning zigzag across the sky.

The first time that any of the sisters had been allowed to swim to the surface, each had been delighted with her freedom and all she had seen. But now that they were grownups and could swim anywhere they wished, they lost interest in wandering far away; after a month or two the world above lost its attraction. When they were away, they longed for their father's castle, declaring it the most beautiful place of all and the only spot where one really felt at home.

Still, many evenings the five sisters would take each other's hands and rise up through the waters. They had voices far lovelier than any human being. When a storm began to rage and a ship was in danger of being wrecked, then the five sisters would swim in front of it and sing about how beautiful it was down at the bottom of the sea. They begged the sailors not to be frightened but to come down to them. The men could not understand the mermaids' songs; they thought it was the wind that was singing. Besides, they would never see the beauty of the world below them, for if a ship sinks the seamen drown, and when they arrive at the mer-king's castle they are dead.

On such evenings, while her sisters swam, hand in hand, up through the water, the youngest princess had to stay below. She would look sadly up after them and feel like crying; but mermaids can't weep and that makes their suffering even deeper and greater.

"Oh, if only I were fifteen," she would sigh. "I know that I shall love the world above, and the human beings who live up there!"

At last she, too, was fifteen!

"Now you are off our hands," said the old dowager queen. "Let me dress you, just as I dressed your sisters." She put a wreath of white lilies around her hair; each of the petals of every flower was half a pearl. She let eight oysters clip themselves on to the little mermaid's tail, so that everyone could see that she was a princess.

"It hurts," said the little mermaid.

"One has to suffer for position," said her old grandmother. The little mermaid would gladly have exchanged her heavy pearl wreath for one of the red flowers from her garden (she thought they suited her much better) but she didn't dare.

"Farewell," she said and rose, light as a bubble, up through the water.

The sun had just set when she lifted her head above the surface. The clouds still had the colour of roses and in the horizon was a fine line of gold; in the pale pink sky the first star of evening sparkled, clearly and beautifully. The air was warm and the sea was calm. She saw a three-masted ship; only one of its sails was unfurled, and it hung motionless in the still air. Up on the yards the sailors sat, looking down upon the deck from which music could be heard. As the evening grew darker, hundreds of little coloured lamps were hung from the rigging; they looked like the flags of all the nations of the world. The little mermaid swam close to a porthole and the swells lifted her gently so that she could look in through it. The great cabin was filled with gaily dressed people; the handsomest among them was a young prince with large, dark eyes. He looked no older than sixteen, and that was, in truth, his age; that very day was his birthday. All the festivities were for him. The sailors danced on the deck, and as the young prince came up to watch them, a hundred rockets flew into the sky.

The night became as bright as day and the little mermaid got so frightened that she ducked down under the water. But she soon stuck her head up again; and then it looked as if all the stars of the heavens were falling down on top of her. She had never seen fireworks before. Pinwheels turned; rockets shot into the air, and their lights reflected in the dark mirror of the sea. The deck of the ship was so illuminated that every rope could clearly be seen. Oh, how handsome the young prince was! He laughed and smiled and shook hands with everyone, while music was played in the still night.

It grew late, but the little mermaid could not turn her eyes away from the ship and the handsome prince. The coloured lamps were put out. No more rockets shot into the air and no more cannons were fired. From the depth of the ocean came a rumbling noise. The little mermaid let the waves be her rocking horse, and they lifted her so that she could look in through the porthole. The ship started to sail faster and faster, as one sail after another was unfurled. Now the waves grew in size and black clouds could be seen on the horizon and far away lightning flashed.

A storm was brewing. The sailors took down the sails. The great ship tossed and rolled in the huge waves that rose as though they were mountains that wanted to bury the ship and break its proud mast. But the ship, like a swan, rode on top of the waves and let them lift her high into

the sky. The little mermaid thought it was very amusing to watch the ship sailing so fast, but the sailors didn't. The ship creaked and groaned; the great planks seemed to bulge as the waves hit them. Suddenly the mast snapped as if it were a reed. It tumbled into the water. The ship heeled over, and the sea broke over it.

Only now did the little mermaid understand that the ship was in danger. She had to be careful herself and keep away from the spars and broken pieces of timber that were being flung by the waves. For a moment it grew so dark that she could see nothing, then a bolt of lightning illuminated the sinking ship. She looked for the young prince among the terrified men on board who were trying to save themselves, but not until that very moment, when the ship finally sank, did she see him.

At first, she thought joyfully, "Now he will come down to me!" But then she remembered that man could not live in the sea and the young prince would be dead when he came to her father's castle.

"He must not die," she thought, and dived in among the wreckage, forgetting the danger that she herself was in, for any one of the great beams that were floating in the turbulent sea could have crushed her.

She found him! He was too tired to swim any farther; he had no more strength in his arms and legs to fight the storm-whipped waves. He closed his eyes, waiting for death, and he would have drowned, had the little mermaid not saved him. She held his head above water and let the waves carry them where they would.

By morning the storm was over. Of the wrecked ship not a splinter was to be found. The sun rose, glowing red, and its rays gave colour to the young prince's cheeks but his eyes remained closed. The little mermaid kissed his forehead and stroked his wet hair. She thought that he looked like the statue in her garden. She kissed him again and wished passionately that he would live.

In the far distance she saw land; the mountains rose blue in the morning air. The snow on their peaks was as glittering white as swan's feathers. At the shore there was a green forest, and in its midst lay a cloister or a church, the little mermaid did not know which. Lemon and orange trees grew in the garden, and by the entrance gate stood a tall palm tree. There was a little bay nearby, where the water was calm and deep. The mermaid swam with her prince towards the beach. She laid him in the fine white sand, taking care to place his head in the warm sunshine far from the water.

In the big white buildings bells were ringing and a group of young girls was coming out to walk in the garden. The little mermaid swam out to some rocks and hid behind them. She covered her head with seaweed, so that she would not be noticed, while she waited to see who would find the poor prince.

Soon one of the young girls discovered him. At first she seemed frightened, and she called the others. Many people came. The prince opened his eyes and smiled up at those who stood around him—not out towards the sea, where the little mermaid was peeping from behind a stone. But then he could not possibly have known that she was there and that it was she who had saved him. The little mermaid felt so terribly sad; the prince was carried into the big white building, and the little mermaid dived down into the sea and swam sorrowfully home to her father's castle.

She had always been quiet and thoughtful. Now she grew even more silent. Her sisters asked her what she had seen on her first visit up above, but she did not answer.

Many mornings and evenings she would swim back to the place where she had last seen the prince. She watched the fruits in the orchard ripen and be picked, and saw the snow on the high mountains melt, but she never saw the prince. She would return from each of these visits a little sadder. She would seek comfort by embracing the statue in her garden, which looked like the prince. She no longer tended her flowers, and they grew into a wilderness, covering the paths and weaving their long stalks and leaves into the branches of the trees, so that it became quite dark down in her garden.

At last she could bear her sorrow no longer and told one of her sisters about it; and almost at once the others knew as well. But no one else was told; that is, except for a couple of other mermaids, but they didn't tell it to anyone except their nearest and dearest friends. It was one of these friends who knew who the prince was. She, too, had seen the birthday party on the ship, and she could tell where he came from and where his kingdom was.

"Come, little sister," the other princesses called, and with their arms around each other's shoulders they swam.

All in a row they rose to the surface when they came to the shore where the prince's castle stood. It was built of glazed yellow stones and had many flights of marble stairs leading up to it. The steps of one of them went all the way down to the sea. Golden domes rose above the roofs, and pillars bore an arcade that went all the way around the palace. Between the pillars stood marble statues; they looked almost as if they were alive. Through the clear glass of the tall windows, one could look into the most beautiful chambers and halls, where silken curtains and tapestries hung on the walls; and there were large paintings that were truly a pleasure to look at. In the largest hall was a fountain. The water shot high up toward the glass cupola in the roof, through which the sunbeams fell on the water and the beautiful flowers that grew in the basin of the fountain.

Now that she knew where the prince lived, the little mermaid spent many evenings and nights looking at the splendid palace. She swam nearer to the land than any of her sisters had ever dared. There was a marble balcony that cast its shadow across a narrow canal, and beneath it she hid and watched the young prince, who thought that he was all alone in the moonlight.

Many an evening she saw the prince sail with his musicians in his beautiful boat. She peeped from behind the tall reeds; and if someone noticed her silver-white veil, they probably thought that they had only seen a swan stretching its wings.

Many a night she heard the fishermen talking to each other and telling about how kind and good the prince was; and she was so glad that she had saved his life when she had found him, half dead, drifting on the waves. She remembered how his head had rested on her chest and with what passion she had kissed him. But he knew nothing about his rescue; he could not even dream about her.

More and more she grew to love human beings and wished that she could leave the sea and live among them. It seemed to her that their world was far larger than hers; on ships, they could sail across the oceans and they could climb the mountains high up above the clouds. Their countries were vast, covered with fields and forests; she knew that they stretched much farther than she could see. There was so much she wanted to know and so few questions her sisters could answer; therefore she went to her old grandmother, who knew much about the "higher world", as she called the lands above the sea.

"If men are not so unlucky as to drown," asked the little mermaid, "then do they live forever? Don't they die as we do, down here in the sea?"

"Yes, they do," answered her grandmother. "Men must also die and their life span is shorter than ours. We can live until we are three hundred years old; but when we die, we become the foam on the ocean. We cannot even bury our loved ones. We do not have immortal souls. When we die, we shall never rise again. We are like the green reeds: once they are cut they will never be green again. But men have souls that live eternally, even after their bodies have become dust. They rise high up into the clear sky where the stars are. As we rise up through the water to look at the world of man, they rise up to the unknown, the beautiful world, that we shall never see."

"Why do I not have an immortal soul!" sighed the little mermaid unhappily. "I would give all my three hundred years of life for only one day as a human being if, afterward, I should be allowed to live in the heavenly world."

"You shouldn't think about things like that," said her old grandmother. "We live far happier down here than man does up there."

"I am going to die, become foam on the ocean, and never again hear the music of the waves or see the flowers and the burning red sun. Can't I do anything to win an immortal soul?"

"No," said the old merwoman. "Only if a man should fall so much in love with you that you were dearer to him than his mother and father; and he cared so much for you that all his thoughts were of his love for you; and he let a priest take his right hand and put it in yours, while he promised to be eternally true to you, then his soul would flow into your body and you would be able to partake of human happiness. He can give you a soul and yet keep his own. But it will never happen. For that which we consider beautiful down here in the ocean, your fishtail, they find ugly up above, on earth. They have no sense; up there, you have to have two clumsy props, which they call legs, in order to be called beautiful."

The little mermaid sighed and glanced sadly down at her fishtail.

"Let us be happy," said her old grandmother. "We can swim and dive among the waves for three hundred years, that is time enough. Tonight we are going to give a court ball in the castle."

Such a splendour did not exist up above on the earth. The walls and the ceilings of the great hall were made of clear glass; four hundred giant green and pink oyster shells stood in rows along the walls. Blue flames rose from them and not only lighted the hall but also illuminated the sea outside. Numberless fishes—both big and small—swam close to the glass walls; some of them had purple scales, others seemed to be of silver and gold. Through the great hall flowed a swiftly moving current, and on that the mermen and mermaids danced, while they sang their own beautiful songs. Such lovely voices are never heard up on earth; and the little mermaid sang most beautifully of them all. The others clapped their hands when she had finished, and for a moment she felt happy, knowing that she had the most beautiful voice both on earth and in the sea.

But soon she started thinking again of the world above. She could not forget the handsome prince, and mourned because she did not have an immortal soul like his. She sneaked out of her father's palace, away from the ball, from the gaiety, down into her little garden.

From afar the sound of music, of horns being played, came down to her through the water; and she thought: "Now he is sailing up there, the prince whom I love more than I love my father and mother: he who is ever in my thoughts and in whose hands I would gladly place all my hope of happiness. I would dare to do anything to win him and an immortal soul! While my sisters are dancing in the palace, I will go to the sea witch, though I have always feared her, and ask her to help me."

The little mermaid swam toward the turbulent maelstrom; beyond it the sea witch lived. In this part of the great ocean the little mermaid had never been before; here no flowers or seaweeds grew, only the grey naked sea bed stretched towards the centre of the maelstrom, that great whirlpool where the water, as if it had been set in motion by gigantic mill wheels, twisted and turned: grinding, tearing, and sucking anything that came within its reach down into its depths. Through this turbulence the little mermaid had to swim, for beyond it lay the bubbling mud flats that the sea witch called her bog and that had to be crossed to come to the place where she lived.

The sea witch's house was in the midst of the strangest forest. The bushes and trees were gigantic polyps that were half plant and half animal. They looked like snakes with hundreds of heads, but they grew out of the ground. Their branches were long slimy arms, and they had fingers as supple as worms; every limb was in constant motion from the root to the utmost point. Everything they could reach they grasped, and never let go of it again. With dread the little mermaid stood at the entrance to the forest; her heart was beating with fear, she almost turned back. But then she remembered her prince and the soul she wanted to gain and her courage returned.

She braided her long hair and bound it around her head, so the polyps could not catch her by it. She held her arms folded tightly across her breast and then she flew through the water as fast as the swiftest fish. The ugly polyps stretched out their arms and their fingers tried to grasp her. She noticed that every one of them was holding, as tightly as iron bands, on to something it had caught. Drowned human beings peeped out as white skeletons among the polyps' arms. There were sea chests, rudders of ships, skeletons of land animals; and then she saw a poor little mermaid who had been caught and strangled; and this sight was to her the most horrible.

At last she came to a great, slimy, open place in the middle of the forest. Big fat eels played in the mud, showing their ugly yellow stomachs. Here the witch had built her house out of the bones of drowned sailors, and there she sat letting a big ugly toad eat out of her mouth, as human beings sometimes let a canary eat sugar candy out of theirs. The ugly eels she called her little chickens, and held them close to her spongy chest.

"I know what you want," she cackled. "And it is stupid of you. But you shall have your wish, for it will bring you misery, little princess. You want to get rid of your fishtail, and instead have two stumps to walk on as human beings have, so that the prince will fall in love with you; and you will gain both him and an immortal soul." The witch laughed so loudly and evilly that the toad and eels she had had on her lap jumped down into the mud.

"You came at the right time," she said. "Tomorrow I could not have helped you; you would have had to wait a year. I will mix you a potion. Drink it tomorrow morning before the sun rises, while you are sitting on the beach. Your tail will divide and shrink until it becomes what human beings call 'pretty legs.' It will hurt; it will feel as if a sword were going through your body. All who see you will say that you are the most beautiful human child they have ever seen. You will walk more gracefully than any dancer; but every time your foot touches the ground it will feel as though you were walking on knives so sharp that your blood must flow. If you are willing to suffer all this, then I can help you."

"I will," whispered the little mermaid, and thought of her prince and how she would win an immortal soul.

"But remember," screeched the witch, "that once you have a human body you can never become a mermaid again. Never again shall you swim through the waters with your sisters to your father's castle. If you cannot make the prince fall so much in love with you that he forgets both his father and mother, because his every thought concerns only you, and he orders the priest to take his right hand and place it in yours, so that you become man and wife; then, the first morning after he has married another, your heart will break and you will become foam on the ocean."

"I still want to try," said the little mermaid, and her face was as white as a corpse.

"But you will have to pay me, too," grinned the witch. "And I want no small payment. You have the most beautiful voice of all those who live in the ocean. I suppose you have thought of using that to charm your prince; but that voice you will have to give to me. I want the most precious thing you have to pay for my potion. It contains my own blood, so that it can be as sharp as a double-edged sword."

"But if you take my voice," said the little mermaid, "what will I have left?"

"Your beautiful body," said the witch. "Your graceful walk and your lovely eyes. Speak with them and you will be able to capture a human heart. Have you lost your courage? Stick out your little tongue, and let me cut it off in payment, and you shall have the potion."

"Let it happen," whispered the little mermaid.

The witch took out a caldron in which to make the magic potion. "Cleanliness is a virtue," she said. And before she put the pot over the fire, she scrubbed it with eels, which she had made into a whisk.

She cut her chest and let her blood drip into the vessel. The steam that rose became strange figures that were terrifying to see. Every minute, the witch put something different into the caldron. When the brew reached a rolling boil, it sounded as though a crocodile were crying. At last the potion was finished. It looked as clear and pure as water.

"Here it is," said the witch, and cut out the little mermaid's tongue. Now she was mute, she could neither speak nor sing.

"If any of the polyps should try to grab you, on your way back through my forest," said the witch, "you need only spill one drop of the potion on it and its arms and fingers will splinter into a thousand pieces."

But the little mermaid didn't have to do that. Fearfully, the polyps drew away when they saw what she was carrying in her hands; the potion sparkled as though it were a star. Safely, she returned through the forest, the bog, and the maelstrom.

She could see her father's palace. The lights were extinguished in the great hall. Everyone was asleep; and yet she did not dare to seek out her sisters; now that she was mute and was going away from them forever. She felt as if her heart would break with sorrow. She sneaked down into

the garden and picked a flower from each of her sisters' gardens; then she threw a thousand finger kisses toward the place and swam upward through the deep blue sea.

The sun had not yet risen when she reached the prince's castle and sat down on the lowest step of the great marble stairs. The moon was still shining clearly. The little mermaid drank the potion and it felt as if a sword were piercing her little body. She fainted and lay as though she were dead.

When the sun's rays touched the sea she woke and felt a burning pain; but the young prince stood in front of her and looked at her with his coal-black eyes. She looked downward and saw then that she no longer had a fishtail but the most beautiful, little, slender legs that any girl could wish for. She was naked; and therefore she took her long hair and covered herself with it.

The prince asked her who she was and how she had got there. Gently and sadly, she looked up at him with her deep blue eyes, for she could not speak. He took her by the hand and led her up to his castle. And just as the witch had warned, every step felt as though she were walking on sharp knives. But she suffered it gladly. Gracefully as a bubble rising in the water, she walked beside the prince; and everyone who saw her wondered how she could walk so lightly.

In the castle, she was clad in royal clothes of silk and muslin. She was the most beautiful of all, but she was mute and could neither sing nor speak. Beautiful slave girls, clad in silken clothes embroidered with gold, sang for the prince and his royal parents. One sang more beautifully than the rest, and the prince clapped his hands and smiled to her; then the little mermaid was filled with sorrow, for she knew that she had once sung far more beautifully. And she thought, "Oh, if he only knew that to be with him I have given away my voice for all eternity."

Now the slave girls danced, gracefully they moved to the beautiful music. Suddenly the little mermaid lifted her hands and rose on the tips of her toes. She floated more than danced across the floor. No one had ever seen anyone dance as she did. Her every movement revealed her loveliness and her eyes spoke far more eloquently than the slave's song.

Everyone was delighted, especially the prince. He called her his little foundling. She danced again and again, even though each time her little foot touched the floor she felt as if she had stepped on a knife. The prince declared that she should never leave him, and she was given permission to sleep in front of his door on a velvet pillow.

The prince had men's clothes made for her, so that she could accompany him when he went horseback riding. Through the sweet-smelling forest they rode, where green branches touched their shoulders and little birds sang among the leaves. Together they climbed the high mountains and her feet bled so much that others noticed it; but she smiled and followed her prince up ever higher until they could see the clouds sail below them, like flocks of birds migrating to foreign lands.

At night in the castle, while the others slept, she would walk down the broad marble stairs to the sea and cool her poor burning feet in the cold water. Then she would think of her sisters, down in the deep sea.

One night they came; arm in arm they rose above the surface of the water, singing mournfully. She waved to them, and they recognized her, and they told her how much sorrow she had brought them. After that they visited her every night; and once she saw, far out to sea, her old grandmother. It had been years since she had stuck her head up into the air; and there, too, was her father the mer-king with his crown on his head. They stretched their hands towards her but did not dare come as near to the land as her sisters.

Day by day the prince grew fonder and fonder of her; but he loved her as he would have loved a good child, and had no thought of making her his queen. And she had to become his wife or she would never have an immortal soul, but on the morning after his marriage would become foam on the great ocean.

"Don't you love me more than you do all others?" was the message in the little mermaid's eyes when the prince kissed her lovely forehead.

"Yes, you are the dearest to me," said the prince, "for you have the kindest heart of them all. You are devoted to me and you look like a young girl I once saw, and will probably never see again. I was in a shipwreck. The waves carried me ashore, where a holy temple lay. Many young girls were in service there; one of them, the youngest of them all, found me on the beach and saved my life. I saw her only twice, but she is the only one I can love in this world; and you look like her. You almost make her picture disappear from my soul. She belongs to the holy temple and, therefore, good fortune has sent you to me instead, and we shall never part."

"Oh, he does not know that it was I who saved his life," thought the little mermaid. "I carried him across the sea to the forest where the temple stood. I hid behind the rocks and watched over him until he was found. I saw that beautiful girl whom he loves more than me!'' And the little mermaid sighed deeply, for cry she couldn't. "He has said that the girl belongs to the holy temple and will never come out into the world, and they will never meet again. But I am with him and see him every day. I will take care of him, love him, and devote my life to him.''

Everyone said that the young prince was to be married; he was to have the neighbouring king's daughter, a beautiful princess. A magnificent ship was built and made ready. It was announced that the prince was travelling to see the neighbouring kingdom, but that no one believed. "It is not the country but the princess he is to inspect,'' they all agreed.

The little mermaid shook her head and smiled; she knew what the prince thought, and they didn't.

"I must go,'' he had told her, "I must look at the beautiful princess, my parents demand it. But they won't force me to carry her home as my bride. I can't love her. She does not look like the girl from the temple as you do. If I ever marry, I shall most likely choose you, my little foundling with the eloquent eyes.'' And he kissed her on her red lips and played with her long hair, and let his head rest so near her heart that it dreamed of human happiness and an immortal soul.

"Are you afraid of the ocean, my little silent child?'' asked the prince as they stood on the deck of the splendid ship that was to sail them to the neighbouring kingdom. He told the little mermaid how the sea can be still or stormy, and about the fishes that live in it, and what the divers had seen underneath the water. She smiled as he talked, for who knew better than she about the world on the bottom of the ocean?

In the moonlit night, when everyone slept but the sailor at the rudder and the lookout in the bow, she sat on the bulwark and looked down into the clear water. She thought she saw her father's palace; and on the top of its tower her old grandmother was standing with her silver crown on her head, looking up through the currents of the sea, toward the keel of the ship. Her sisters came; they looked at her so sorrowfully and wrung their white hands in despair; she waved to them and smiled. She wanted them to know that she was happy, but just at that moment the little cabin boy came and her sisters dived down under the water; he saw nothing but some white foam on the ocean.

The next morning the ship sailed into the harbour of the great town that belonged to the neighbouring king. All the church bells were ringing, and from the tall towers trumpets blew, while the soldiers stood at attention, with banners flying and bayonets on their rifles.

Every day another banquet was held, and balls and parties followed one after the other. But the princess attended none of them, for she did not live in the palace; she was being educated in the holy temple, where she was to learn all the royal virtues.

At last she came! No one was more eager to see her than the little mermaid; and when she finally did, she had to admit that a more beautiful girl she had never seen before. Her skin was so delicate and fine, and beneath her long dark lashes smiled a pair of faithful, dark blue eyes.

"It is you!" exclaimed the prince. "You are the one who saved me, when I lay half dead on the beach!" And he embraced his blushing bride.

"Oh, now I am too happy," he said to the little mermaid. "That which I never dared hope has now happened! You will share my joy, for I know that you love me more than any of the others do."

The little mermaid kissed his hand; she felt as if her heart were breaking. His wedding morning would bring her death and she would be changed into foam.

All the churchbells rang and heralds rode through the streets and announced the wedding to the people. On all the altars costly silver lamps burned with fragrant oils. The priests swung censers with burning incense in them, while the prince and the princess gave each other their hands, and the bishop blessed them. The little mermaid, dressed in silk and gold, held the train of the bride's dress, but her ears did not hear the music, nor did her eyes see the holy ceremony, for this night would bring her death, and she was thinking of all she had lost in this world.

The bride and bridegroom embarked upon the prince's ship; cannons saluted and banners flew. On the main deck, a tent of gold and scarlet cloth had been raised; there on the softest of pillows the bridal couple would sleep.

The sails were unfurled, and they swelled in the wind and the ship glided across the transparent sea.

When it darkened and evening came, coloured lamps were lit and the sailors danced on the deck. The little mermaid could not help remembering the first time she had emerged above the waves, when she had seen the almost identical sight. She whirled in the dance, glided as the swallow does in the air when it is pursued. Everyone cheered and applauded her. Never had she danced so beautifully; the sharp knives cut her feet, but she did not feel it, for the pain in her heart was far greater. She knew that this was the last evening that she would see him for whose sake she had given away her lovely voice and left her home and her family; and he would never know of her sacrifice. It was the last night that she would breathe the same air as he, or look out over the deep sea and up into the star-blue heaven. A dreamless, eternal night awaited her, for she had no soul and had not been able to win one.

Until midnight all was gaiety aboard the ship, and the mermaid danced and laughed with the thought of death in her heart. Then the prince kissed his bride and she fondled his long black hair and, arm in arm, they walked into their splendorous tent, to sleep.

The ship grew quiet. Only the sailor at the helm and the little mermaid were awake. She stood with her white arms resting on the railing and looked towards the east. She searched the horizon for the pink of dawn; she knew that the first sunbeams would kill her.

Out of the sea rose her sisters, but the wind could no longer play with their long beautiful hair, for their heads had been shorn.

"We have given our hair to the sea witch, so that she would help you and you would not have to die this night. Here is a knife that the witch has given us. Look how sharp it is! Before the sun rises, you must plunge it into the heart of the prince; when his warm blood sprays on your feet, they will turn into a fishtail and you will be a mermaid again. You will be able to live your three hundred years down in the sea with us, before you die and become foam on the ocean. Hurry! He or you must die before the sun rises. Our grandmother mourns; she, too, has no hair; hers has fallen out from grief. Kill the prince and come back to us! Hurry! See, there is a pink haze on the horizon. Soon the sun will rise and you will die."

The little mermaid heard the sound of her sisters' deep and strange sighing before they disappeared beneath the waves.

She pulled aside the crimson cloth of the tent and saw the beautiful bride sleeping peacefully, with her head resting on the prince's chest. The little mermaid bent down and kissed his handsome forehead. She turned and looked at the sky; more and more, it was turning red. She glanced at the sharp knife; and once more she looked down at the prince. He moved a little in his sleep and whispered the name of his bride. Only she was in his thoughts, in his dreams! The little mermaid's hand trembled as it squeezed the handle of the knife, then she threw the weapon into the sea. The waves turned red where it fell, as if drops of blood were seeping up through the water.

Again she looked at the prince; her eyes were already glazed in death. She threw herself into the sea and felt her body changing into foam.

The sun rose out of the sea, its rays felt warm and soft on the deathly cold foam. But the little mermaid did not feel death, she saw the sun, and up above her floated hundreds of airy, transparent forms. She could see right through them, see the sails of the ship and the blood-red clouds. Their voices were melodious, but so muted that no human ear could hear them, just as their forms were so fragile that no human eye could see them. So light were they that they glided through the air, though they had no wings. The little mermaid looked down and saw that she was like them.

"Where am I?" she asked; and her voice sounded like theirs—so lovely and so melodious that no human music could reproduce it.

"We are the daughters of the air," they answered. "Mermaids have no immortal soul and can never have one, unless they can obtain the love of a human being. Their chance of obtaining eternal life depends upon others. We, daughters of the air, have not received an eternal soul either; but we can win one by good deeds. We fly to the warm countries, where the heavy air of the plague rests, and blow cool winds to spread it. We carry the smell of flowers that refresh and heal the sick. If for three hundred years we earnestly try to do what is good, we obtain an immortal soul and can take part in the eternal happiness of man. You, little mermaid, have tried with all your heart to do the same. You have suffered and borne your suffering bravely; and that is why you are now among us, the spirits of the air. Do your good deeds and in three hundred years an immortal soul will be yours."

The little mermaid lifted her arms up towards God's sun, and for the first time she felt a tear.

She heard noise coming from the ship. She saw the prince and the princess searching for her. Sadly they looked at the sea, as if they knew that she had thrown herself into the waves. Without being seen, she kissed the bride's forehead and smiled at the prince; then she rose together with the other children of the air, up into a pink cloud that was sailing by.

"In three hundred years I shall rise like this into God's kingdom," she said.

"You may be able to go there before that," whispered one of the others to her. "Invisibly, we fly through the homes of human beings. They can't see us, so they don't know when we are there; but if we find a good child, who makes his parents happy and deserves their love, we smile and God takes a year away from the time of our trial. But if there is a naughty and mean child in the house we come to, we cry; and for every tear we shed God adds a day to the three hundred years we already must serve."

The Red Shoes

Once there was a little girl who was delicate and lovely but very poor. In the summer she had to go barefoot and in the winter she had to wear wooden shoes that rubbed against her poor little ankles and made them red and sore.

In the same village there lived an old widow whose husband had been a shoemaker; and she was sewing a pair of shoes from scraps of red material. She did her very best, but the shoes looked a bit clumsy, though they were sewn with kindness. They were meant for the poor little girl, whose name was Karen.

Now on that very day that her mother was to be buried, Karen was given the red shoes. Though they weren't the proper colour for mourning, she had no others, so she put them on. Raggedly dressed, bare-legged, with red shoes on her feet, she walked behind the pauper's coffin.

A big old-fashioned carriage drove by; in it sat an old lady. She noticed the little girl and felt so sorry for her that she went at once to the minister and spoke to him. "Let me have that little girl, and I shall be good to her and bring her up."

Karen thought it was because of her new red shoes that the old lady had taken a fancy to her. But the old lady declared that the shoes looked frightful and had them thrown into the stove and burned. Karen was dressed in nice clean clothes and taught to read and to sew. Everyone agreed that she was a very pretty child; but the mirror said, "You are more than pretty, you are beautiful."

It happened that the queen was making a journey throughout the country, and she had her daughter, the little princess, with her. Everywhere people streamed to see them. When they arrived at a castle near Karen's village, the little girl followed the crowd out there. Looking out of one of the great windows of the castle was the little princess. So that people could see her, she was standing on a little stool. She had no crown on her head but she wore a very pretty white dress and the loveliest red shoes, made from morocco. They were certainly much prettier than the ones the old shoemaker's widow had made for Karen. But even they had been red shoes, and to Karen nothing else in the world was so desirable.

Karen became old enough to be confirmed. She was to have a new dress and new shoes for this solemn occasion. The old lady took her to the finest shoemaker in the nearby town and he measured her little foot. Glass cabinets filled with the most elegant shoes and boots covered the walls of his shop. But the old lady's eyesight was so poor that she didn't get much out of looking at the display. Karen did; between two pairs of boots stood a pair of red shoes just like the ones the princess had worn. Oh, how beautiful they were! The shoemaker said that they had been made for the daughter of a count but that they hadn't fitted her.

"I think they are patent leather," remarked the old lady. "They shine."

"Yes, they shine!" sighed Karen as she tried them on. They fitted the child and the old woman bought them. Had she known that they were red, she wouldn't have because it was not proper to wear red shoes when you were being confirmed. But her eyesight was failing—poor woman!—and she had not seen the colour.

Everyone in the church looked at Karen's feet, as she walked towards the altar. On the walls of the church hung paintings of the former ministers and their wives who were buried there; they were portrayed wearing black with white ruffs around their necks. Karen felt that even they were staring at her red shoes.

When the old bishop laid his hands on her head and spoke of the solemn promise she was about to make—of her covenant with God to be a good Christian—her mind was not on his words. The ritual music was played on the organ; the old cantor sang, and the sweet voices of the children could be heard, but Karen was thinking of her red shoes.

By afternoon, everyone had told the old lady about the colour of

Karen's shoes. She was very angry and scolded the girl, telling her how improper it was to have worn red shoes in church, and that she must remember always to wear black ones, even if she had to put on an old pair.

Next Sunday Karen was to attend communion. She looked at her black shoes and she looked at her red shoes; then she looked at her red shoes once more and put them on.

The sun was shining, it was a beautiful day. The old lady and Karen took the path across the fields and their shoes got a bit dirty.

At the entrance to the church stood an old invalid soldier leaning on a crutch. He had a marvellously long beard that was red with touches of white in it. He bowed low towards the old lady and asked her permission to wipe the dust off her feet. Karen put her little foot forward too.

"What pretty little dancing shoes!" said the soldier and, tapping them on the soles, he added, "Remember to stay on her feet for the dance."

The old lady gave the soldier a penny, and she and Karen entered the church.

Again everyone looked at Karen's feet, even the people in the paintings on the wall. When she knelt in front of the altar and the golden cup was lifted to her lips, she thought only of the red shoes and saw them reflected in the wine. She did not join in the singing of the psalm and she forgot to say the Lord's Prayer.

The coachman had come with the carriage to drive them home from church. The old lady climbed in and Karen was about to follow her when the old soldier, who was standing nearby, remarked, "Look at those pretty dancing shoes."

His words made her take a few dancing steps. Once she had begun, her feet would not stop. It was as if the shoes had taken command of them. She danced around the corner of the church; her will was not her own.

The coachman jumped off the carriage and ran after her. When he finally caught up with her, he grabbed her and lifted her up from the ground, but her feet kept on dancing in the air, even after he managed to get her into the carriage. The poor old woman was kicked nastily while she and the coachman took Karen's shoes off her feet, so she could stop dancing.

When they got home, the red shoes were put away in a cupboard, but Karen could not help sneaking in to look at them.

The old lady was very ill. The doctors had come and said that she would not live much longer. She needed careful nursing and constant care, and who else but Karen ought to give it to her? In the town there was to be a great ball and Karen had been invited to go. She looked at the old lady, who was going to die anyway, and then she glanced at her red shoes. To glance was no sin. Then she put them on; that too did no great harm. But she went to the ball!

She danced! But when she wanted to dance to the left, the shoes danced to the right; and when she wanted to dance up the ballroom floor, the shoes danced right down the stairs and out into the street. Dance she did, out through the city gates and into the dark forest.

Something shone through the trees. She thought it was the moon because it had a face. But it was not; it was the old soldier with the red beard. He nodded to her and exclaimed, "Look what beautiful dancing shoes!"

Terrified, she tried to pull off her shoes. She tore her stockings but the shoes stayed on. They had grown fast to her feet. Dance she did! And dance she must! Over the fields and meadows, in the rain and sunshine, by night and by day. But it was more horrible and frightening at night when the world was dark.

She danced through the gates of the churchyard; but the dead did not dance with her, they had better things to do. She wanted to sit down on the pauper's grave, where the bitter herbs grew, but for her there was no rest. The church door was open and she danced towards it, but an angel, dressed in white, who had on his back great wings that reached almost to the ground, barred her entrance.

His face was stern and grave, and in his hand he held a broad, shining sword.

"You shall dance," he said, "dance in your red shoes until you become pale and thin. Dance till the skin on your face turns yellow and clings to your bones as if you were a skeleton. Dance you shall from door to door, and when you pass a house where proud and vain children live, there you shall knock on the door so that they will see you and fear your fate. Dance, you shall dance. . . . Dance!"

"Mercy!" screamed Karen, but heard not what the angel answered, for her red shoes carried her away, down through the churchyard, over the meadows, along the highways, through the lanes: always dancing.

One morning she danced past a house that she knew well. From inside she heard psalms being sung. The door opened and a coffin decked with flowers was carried out. The old lady who had been so kind to her was

dead. Now she felt that she was forsaken by all of mankind and cursed by God's angel.

Dance she must, and dance she did. The shoes carried her across fields and meadows, through nettles and briars that tore her feet so they bled.

One morning she danced across the lonely heath until she came to a solitary cottage. Here, she knew, the executioner lived. With her fingers she tapped on his window.

"Come out! Come out!" she called. "I cannot come inside, for I must dance."

The executioner opened his door and came outside. When he saw Karen he said, "Do you know who I am? I am the one who cuts off the heads of evil men; and I can feel my axe beginning to quiver now."

"Do not cut off my head," begged Karen, "for then I should not be able to repent. But cut off my feet!"

She confessed her sins and the executioner cut off her feet, and the red shoes danced away with them into the dark forest. The executioner carved a pair of wooden feet for her and made her a pair of crutches. He taught her the psalm that a penitent sings. She kissed the hand that had guided the axe and went on her way.

"Now I have suffered enough because of those red shoes," thought Karen. "I shall go to church now and be among other people."

But when she walked up to the door of the church, the red shoes danced in front of her, and in horror she fled.

All during that week she felt sad and cried many a bitter tear. When Sunday came she thought, "Now I have suffered and struggled long enough. I am just as good as many of those who are sitting and praying in church right now, and who dare to throw their heads back with pride." This reasoning gave her courage, but she came no farther than the gate of the churchyard. There were the shoes dancing in front of her. In terror she fled, but this time she really repented in the depth of her heart.

She went to the minister's house and begged to be given work. She said that she did not care about wages but only wanted a roof over her head and enough to eat. The minister's wife hired the poor cripple because she felt sorry for her. Karen was grateful that she had been given a place to live and she worked hard. In the evening when the minister read from the Bible, she sat and listened thoughtfully. The children were fond of her and she played with them, but when they talked of finery and being beautiful like a princess, she would sadly shake her head.

When Sunday came, everyone in the household got ready for church, and they asked her to go with them. Poor Karen's eyes filled with tears. She sighed and glanced towards her crutches.

When the others had gone, she went into her little room that was so small that a bed and a chair were all it could hold. She sat down and began to read from her psalmbook. The wind carried the music from the church organ down to her, and she lifted her tear-stained face and whispered, "Oh, God, help me!"

Suddenly the sunlight seemed doubly bright and an angel of God stood before her. He was the same angel who with his sword had barred her entrance to the church, but now he held a rose branch covered with flowers. With this he touched the low ceiling of the room and it rose high into the air and, where he had touched it, a golden star shone. He touched the walls and they widened.

Karen saw the organ. She saw the old paintings of the ministers and their wives; and there were the congregation holding their psalmbooks in front of them and singing. The church had come to the poor girl in her little narrow chamber; or maybe she had come to the church. Now she sat among the others, and when they finished singing the psalm they looked up and saw her.

Someone whispered to her: "It is good that you came, Karen."

"This is His mercy," she replied.

The great organ played and the voices of the children in the choir mingled sweetly with it. The clear, warm sunshine streamed through the window. The sunshine filled Karen's heart till it so swelled with peace and happiness that it broke. Her soul flew on a sunbeam up to God; and up there no one asked her about the red shoes.

Inchelina

Once upon a time there was a woman whose only desire was to have a tiny little child. Now she had no idea where she could get one; so she went to an old witch and asked her: "Please, could you tell me where I could get a tiny little child? I would so love to have one."

"That is not so difficult," said the witch. "Here is a grain of barley; it is not the kind that grows in the farmer's fields or that you can feed to the chickens. Plant it in a flowerpot and watch what happens."

"Thank you," said the woman. She handed the witch twelve pennies, and she went home to plant the grain of barley. No sooner was it in the earth than it started to sprout. A beautiful big flower grew up; it looked like a tulip that was just about to bloom.

"What a lovely flower," said the woman, and kissed the red and yellow petals that were closed so tightly. With a snap they opened and one could see that it was a real tulip. In the centre of the flower on the green stigma sat a tiny little girl. She was so beautiful and so delicate, and exactly one inch long. "I will call her Inchelina," thought the woman.

The lacquered shell of a walnut became Inchelina's cradle, the blue petals of violets her mattress, and a rose petal her cover. Here she slept at night; in the daytime she played on the table by the window. The woman had put a bowl of water there with a garland of flowers around it. In this tiny "lake" there floated a tulip petal, on which Inchelina could row from one side of the plate to the other, using two white horsehairs as oars; it was an exquisite sight. And Inchelina could sing, as no one has ever sung before—so clearly and delicately.

One night as she lay sleeping in her beautiful little bed a toad came into the room through a broken windowpane. The toad was big and wet and ugly; she jumped down upon the table where Inchelina was sleeping under her red rose petal.

"She would make a lovely wife for my son," said the toad; and grabbing the walnut shell in which Inchelina slept, she leaped through the broken window and down into the garden.

On the banks of a broad stream, just where it was muddiest, lived the toad with her son. He had taken after his mother and was very ugly. "Croak . . . Croak . . . Croak!" was all he said when he saw the beautiful little girl in the walnut shell.

"Don't talk so loud or you will wake her," scolded the mother. "She could run away and we wouldn't be able to catch her, for she is as light as the down of a swan. I will put her on a water-lily leaf, it will be just like an island to her. In the meantime, we shall get your house, down in the mud, ready for your marriage."

Out in the stream grew many water lilies, and all of their leaves looked as if they were floating in the water. The biggest of them was the farthest from shore; on that one the old toad put Inchelina's little bed.

When the poor little girl woke in the morning and saw where she was—on a green leaf with water all around her—she began to cry bitterly. There was no way of getting to shore at all.

The old toad was very busy down in her mud house, decorating the walls with reeds and yellow flowers that grew near the shore. She meant to do her best for her new daughter-in-law. After she had finished, she and her ugly son swam out to the water-lily leaf to fetch Inchelina's bed. It was to be put in the bridal chamber. The old toad curtsied and that is not easy to do while you are swimming; then she said, "Here is my son. He is to be your husband; you two will live happily down in the mud."

"Croak! . . . Croak!" was all the son said. Then they took the bed and swam away with it. Poor Inchelina sat on the green leaf and wept and wept, for she did not want to live with the ugly toad and have her hideous son as a husband. The little fishes that were swimming about in the brook had heard what the old toad said; they stuck their heads out of the water to take a look at the tiny girl. When they saw how beautiful she was, it hurt them to think that she should have to marry the ugly toad and live in the mud. They decided that they would not let it happen, and gathered around the green stalk that held the leaf anchored to the bottom of the stream. They all nibbled on the stem, and soon the leaf was free. It drifted down the stream, bearing Inchelina far away from the ugly toad.

As Inchelina sailed by, the little birds on the shore saw her and sang, "What a lovely little girl." Farther and farther sailed the leaf with its little passenger, taking her on a journey to foreign lands.

For a long time a lovely white butterfly flew around her, then landed on the leaf. It had taken a fancy to Inchelina. The tiny girl laughed, for she was so happy to have escaped the toad; and the stream was so beautiful, golden in the sunshine. She took the little silk ribbon which she wore around her waist and tied one end of it to the butterfly and the other to the water-lily leaf. Now the leaf raced down the stream—and so did Inchelina, for she was standing on it.

At that moment a big May bug flew by; when it spied Inchelina, it swooped down and with its claws grabbed the poor girl around her tiny waist and flew up into a tree with her. The leaf floated on down the stream, and the butterfly had to follow it.

Oh God, little Inchelina was terrified as the May bug flew away with her, but stronger than her fear was her grief for the poor little white butterfly that she had chained to the leaf with her ribbon. If he did not get loose, he would starve to death.

The May bug didn't care what happened to the butterfly. He placed Inchelina on the biggest leaf on the tree. He gave her honey from the flowers to eat, and told her that she was the loveliest thing he had ever seen, even though she didn't look like a May bug. Soon all the other May bugs that lived in the tree came visiting. Two young lady May bugs—they were still unmarried—wiggled their antennae and said: "She has only two legs, how wretched! No antennae and a thin waist, how disgusting! She looks like a human being: how ugly!"

All the other female May bugs agreed with them. The May bug who had caught Inchelina still thought her lovely; but when all the others kept insisting that she was ugly, he soon was convinced of it too. Now he didn't want her any longer, and put her down on a daisy at the foot of the tree and told her she could go wherever she wanted to, for all he cared. Poor Inchelina cried; she thought it terrible to be so ugly that even a May bug would not want her, and that in spite of her being more beautiful than you can imagine, more lovely than the petal of the most beautiful rose.

All summer long poor Inchelina lived all alone in the forest. She wove a hammock out of grass and hung it underneath a dock leaf so that it would not rain on her while she slept. She ate the honey in the flowers and drank the dew that was on their leaves every morning.

Summer and autumn passed. But then came winter: the long, cold winter. All the birds that had sung so beautifully flew away. The flowers withered, the trees lost their leaves; and the dock leaf that had protected her rolled itself up and became a shrivelled yellow stalk. She was so terribly cold. Her clothes were in shreds; and she was so thin and delicate.

Poor Inchelina, she was bound to freeze to death. It started to snow and each snowflake that fell on her was like a whole shovelful of snow would be to us, because we are so big, and she was only one inch tall.

She wrapped herself in a wizened leaf, but it gave no warmth and she shivered from the cold.

Not far from the forest was a big field where grain had grown; only a few dry stubbles still rose from the frozen ground, pointing up to the heavens. To Inchelina these straws were like a forest. Trembling, she wandered through them and came to the entrance of a field mouse's house. It was only a little hole in the ground. But deep down below the mouse lived in warmth and comfort, with a full larder and a nice kitchen. Like a beggar child, Inchelina stood outside the door and begged for a single grain of barley. It was several days since she had last eaten.

"Poor little wretch," said the field mouse, for she had a kind heart. "Come down into my warm living room and dine with me."

The field mouse liked Inchelina. "You can stay the winter," she said, "But you must keep the room tidy and tell me a story every day, for I like a good story." Inchelina did what the kind old mouse demanded, and she lived quite happily.

"Soon we shall have a visitor," said the mouse. "Once a week my neighbour comes. He lives even more comfortably than I do. He has a drawing room, and wears the most exquisite black fur coat. If only he would marry you, then you would be well provided for. He can't see you, for he is blind, so you will have to tell him the very best of your stories."

But Inchelina did not want to marry the mouse's neighbour, for he was a mole. The next day he came visiting, dressed in his black velvet fur coat. The field mouse said that he was both rich and wise. His house was twenty times as big as hers, and he was cultured, too. But he did not like the sun nor the beautiful flowers, he said they were "abominable," for he had never seen them. Inchelina had to sing for him; and when she sang "*Frère Jacques, dormez vous?*" he fell in love with her because of her beautiful voice; but he didn't show it, for he was sober-minded and never made a spectacle of himself.

He had recently dug a passage from his own house to theirs, and he invited Inchelina and the field mouse to use it as often as they pleased. He told them not to be afraid of the dead bird in the corridor. It had died only a few days before. It was still whole and had all its feathers. By chance it had been buried in his passageway.

The mole took a piece of dry rotten wood in his mouth; it shone as brightly as fire in the darkness; then he led the way down through the long corridor. When they came to the place where the dead bird lay, the mole made a hole with his broad nose, up through the earth, so that light could come through. Almost blocking the passageway was a dead swallow, with its beautiful wings pressed close to its body, its feet almost hidden by feathers, and its head nestled under a wing. The poor bird undoubtedly had frozen to death. Inchelina felt a great sadness; she had loved all the birds that twittered and sang for her that summer. The mole kicked the bird with one of his short legs and said, "Now it has stopped chirping. What a misfortune it is to be born a bird. Thank God, none of my children will be born birds! All they can do is chirp, and then die of starvation when winter comes."

"Yes, that's what all sensible people think," said the field mouse. "What does all that chirping lead to? Starvation and cold when winter comes. But I suppose they think it is romantic."

Inchelina didn't say anything, but when the mouse and mole had their backs turned, she leaned down and kissed the closed eye of the swallow. "Maybe that was one of the birds that sang so beautifully for me this summer," she thought. "How much joy you gave me, beautiful little bird."

The mole closed the hole through which the daylight had entered and then escorted the ladies home. That night Inchelina could not sleep; she rose and wove as large a blanket as she could, out of hay. She carried it down the dark passage and covered the little bird with it. In the field mouse's living room she had found bits of cotton; she tucked them under the swallow wherever she could, to protect it from the cold earth.

"Good-bye, beautiful bird," she said. "Good-bye, and thank you for

the songs you sang for me when it was summer and all the trees were green and the sun warmed us."

She put her head on the bird's breast; then she jumped up! Something was ticking inside: it was the bird's heart, for the swallow was not really dead, and now the warmth had revived it.

In the autumn all the swallows fly to the warm countries. If one tarries too long and is caught by the first frost, he lies down on the ground as if he were dead, and the cold snow covers him.

Inchelina shook with fear. The swallow was huge to a girl so tiny that she only measured an inch. But she gathered her courage and pressed the blanket closer to the bird's body. She even went to fetch the little mint leaf that she herself used as a cover and put it over the bird's head.

The next night she sneaked down to the passageway again; the bird was better although still very weak. He opened his eyes just long enough to see Inchelina standing in the dark with a little piece of dry rotten wood in her hand, as a lamp.

"Thank you, you sweet little child," said the sick swallow, "I feel so much better. I am not cold now. Soon I shall be strong again and can fly out into the sunshine."

"Oh no," she said. "It is cold and snowing outside now and you would freeze. Stay down here in your warm bed, I will nurse you."

She brought the swallow water on a leaf. After he had drunk it, he told her his story. He had torn his wing on a rosebush, and therefore could not fly as swiftly as the other swallows, so he had stayed behind when the others left; then one morning he had fainted from cold. That was all he could remember. He did not know how he came to be in the mole's passageway.

The bird stayed all winter. Inchelina took good care of him, grew very fond of him, and breathed not a word about him to either the mole or the field mouse, for she knew that they didn't like the poor swallow.

As soon as spring came and the warmth of the sun could be felt through the earth, the swallow said good-bye to Inchelina, who opened the hole that the mole had made. The sun shone down so pleasantly. The swallow asked her if she did not want to come along with him; she could sit on his back and he would fly with her out into the great forest. But Inchelina knew that the field mouse would be sad and lonely if she left.

"I cannot," she said.

The bird thanked her once more. "Farewell. . . . Farewell, lovely girl," he sang, and flew out into the sunshine.

Inchelina's eyes filled with tears as she watched the swallow fly away, for she cared so much for the bird.

"Tweet . . . tweet," he sang, and disappeared in the forest.

Poor Inchelina was miserable. Soon the grain would be so tall that the field would be in shade, and she would no longer be able to enjoy the warm sunshine.

"This summer you must spend getting your trousseau ready," said the field mouse, for the sober mole in the velvet coat had proposed to her. "You must have both woollens and linen to wear and to use in housekeeping when you become Mrs. Mole."

Inchelina had to spin by hand and the field mouse hired four spiders to weave both night and day. Every evening the mole came visiting, but all he talked about was how nice it would be when the summer was over. He didn't like the way the sun baked the earth; it made it so hard to dig in. As soon as autumn came they would get married. But Inchelina was not happy; she thought the mole was dull and she did not love him. Every day, at sunrise and at sunset, she tiptoed to the entrance of the field mouse's house, so that when the wind blew and parted the grain, she could see the blue sky above her. She thought of how light and beautiful it was out there, and she longed for her friend the swallow. "He is probably far away in the wonderful green forest!" she thought. "And he will never come back."

Autumn came and Inchelina's trousseau was finished.

"In four weeks we shall hold your wedding," said the field mouse.

Inchelina cried and said she did not want to marry the boring old mole.

"Fiddlesticks!" squeaked the field mouse. "Don't be stubborn or I will bite you with my white teeth. You are getting an excellent husband; he has a velvet coat so fine that the queen does not have one that is better. He has both a larder and kitchen, you ought to thank God for giving you such a good husband."

The day of the wedding came; the mole had already arrived. Inchelina grieved. Now she would never see the warm sun again. The mole lived far down under the ground, for he didn't like the sun. While she lived with the field mouse, she at least had been allowed to walk as far as the entrance of the little house and look at the sun.

"Farewell. . . . Farewell, you beautiful sun!" Inchelina lifted her hands up toward the sky and then took a few steps out upon the field. The harvest was over and only the stubbles were left. She saw a little red flower. Embracing it, she said: "Farewell! And give my love to the swallow if you ever see him."

"Tweet . . . Tweet . . . " something said in the air above her.

She looked up. It was the little swallow. As soon as he saw Inchelina he chirped with joy. And she told the bird how she had to marry the awful .mole, and live forever down under the ground, and never see the sun again. The very telling of her future brought tears to her eyes.

"Now comes the cold winter," said the swallow, "and I fly far away to the warm countries. Why don't you come with me? You can sit on my back; tie yourself on so you won't fall off and we will fly far away from the ugly mole and his dismal house; across the great mountains, to the countries where the sun shines more beautifully than here and the loveliest flowers grow and it is always summer. Fly with me, Inchelina. You saved my life when I lay freezing in the cold cellar of the earth."

"Yes, I will come," cried Inchelina, and climbed up on the bird's back. She tied herself with a ribbon to one of his feathers, and the swallow flew high up into the air, above the forests and lakes and over the high mountains that are always snow-covered. Inchelina froze in the cold air, but she crawled underneath the warm feathers of the bird and only stuck her little head out to see all the beauty below her.

They came to the warm countries. And it was true what the swallow had said: the sun shone more brightly and the sky seemed twice as high. Along the fences grew the loveliest green and blue grapes. From the trees in the forests hung oranges and lemons. Along the roads the most beautiful children ran, chasing many-coloured butterflies. The swallow flew even farther south, and the landscape beneath them became more and more beautiful.

Near a forest, on the shores of a lake, stood the ruins of an ancient temple; ivy wound itself around the white pillars. On top of these were many swallows' nests and one of them belonged to the little swallow that was carrying Inchelina.

"This is my house," he said. "Now choose for yourself one of the beautiful flowers down below and I will set you down on it. It will make a lovely home for you."

"How wonderful!" exclaimed Inchelina, and clapped her hands. Among the broken white marble pillars grew tall, lovely white flowers. The swallow sat her down on the leaves of one of them; and to Inchelina's astonishment, she saw a little man sitting in the centre of the flower. He

was white and almost transparent, as if he were made of glass. On his head he wore a golden crown. On his back were a pair of wings. He was no taller than Inchelina. In every one of the flowers there lived such a tiny angel; and this one was the king of them all.

"How handsome he is!" whispered Inchelina to the swallow.

The tiny little king was terrified of the bird, who was several times larger than he was. But when he saw Inchelina he forgot his fear. She was the loveliest creature he had ever seen; and so he took the crown off his own head and put it on hers. Then he asked her what her name was and whether she wanted to be queen of the flowers.

Now here was a better husband than old mother toad's ugly son or the mole with the velvet coat. Inchelina said yes; and from every flower came a lovely little angel to pay homage to their queen. How lovely and delicate they all were; and they brought her gifts, and the best of these was a pair of wings, so she would be able to fly, as they all did, from flower to flower.

It was a day of happiness. And the swallow, from his nest in the temple, sang for them as well as he could. But in his heart he was sad, for he, too, loved Inchelina and had hoped never to be parted from her.

"You shall not be called Inchelina any longer," said the king. "It is an ugly name. From now on we shall call you Maja."

"Farewell! Farewell!" called the little swallow. He flew back to the north, away from the warm countries. He came to Denmark; and there he has his nest, above the window of a man who can tell fairy tales.

"Tweet . . . tweet," sang the swallow. And the man heard it and wrote down the whole story.